DEATH OF A MOVIE STAR

Timothy Patrick

ISBN: 0989354431
ISBN-13: 9780989354431
Library of Congress Control Number: 2017919089
Country Scribbler
Santa Rosa Valley, CA

Also by Timothy Patrick:

Tea Cups & Tiger Claws

DEDICATION

For my daughter, Alina

CHAPTER ONE

Everyone gets a free murder. It's like a savings bond given to a newborn baby. The only catch is that it takes eighty years to mature. At that age, or anytime thereafter, you are free to commit the murder of your choice. And then, faster than you can say, "rip-roaring-rigor-mortis," your special privileges begin accruing. At arraignment your advanced age and various medical conditions are noted. The judge looks at you, and your oxygen tank, and says something benignly humorous about your flight-risk probability. You are then released on personal recognizance. The district attorney isn't terribly excited because convicting frail, elderly murderers doesn't seem to impress voters as much as convicting young, menacing ones. Better for everyone if you and your crime just quietly fade away. Your numerous continuance requests, therefore, are met with less than vigorous resistance, and your trial is postponed four, five, or even six years. During this time you live peacefully in your own home, which, given an average life expectancy of seventy-eight years, is also where you will die long before the lethargic arm of justice ever comes to gather you up.

Eighty-seven-year-old Lenora Danmore had been willing to exercise this privilege. It was true, the initial scandal might have damaged her reputation, and that of her museum, but over time, the pall of murder would have most likely fallen away and left nothing but a captivating dark passion to her life story, a touch of infamy adorning a remarkable fame, and her reputation would have recovered. But then a chubby Italian actress by the name of Brandi Bonacore came along, and Lenora realized that while a free murder is all fine and good, a perfect murder is even better.

This was the reason Lenora had traveled the sixty miles from her ranch in the foothills above Ventura, California, to a strip-mall diner in Studio City on a blustery day in January 2020. She wore a cream-colored Ralph Lauren pinstriped skirt suit with an upturned collar and matching gloves. The booth where she sat smelled like ketchup. She touched as little as possible.

"Sorry, lady, you gotta move. This section is...Miss Danmore? Uh...I'm sorry...uh...I didn't know it was you. This is such a great honor...What can I get for you?"

Lenora sized up Brandi and her bulging mustard-yellow uniform. Twenty years in Hollywood, and she had landed back at the diner like a newbie. The whole thing was just so perfect.

"Who do you hate?" said Lenora, with an icy, intimidating smile.

"Excuse me, ma'am?"

"Who do you hate?"

"Nobody."

"What happens when you see her face on the side of a passing bus? Or you turn on the TV, and she smiles innocently and tries to sell you beauty lotion?" asked Lenora.

"I don't know what you're talking about," said Brandi.

Now she had started to squirm. Lenora continued: "There are two ways for you to make it to *StarBash*: scandal or drama, and scandal isn't your strength, Brandi."

"Are you sure you got the right lady? I just got rejected by *StarBash*...for the third time."

"Maybe we made a mistake with that rejection."

"Really?"

"I said maybe. It all boils down to scandal and drama."

"Are you kidding me! I got drama comin' out my ass!" said Brandi.

"Yes, I believe you do. Now tell me, when God is far away, and your mind wanders in the darkness, whose dead body do you see?"

"I see Cass Moreaux."

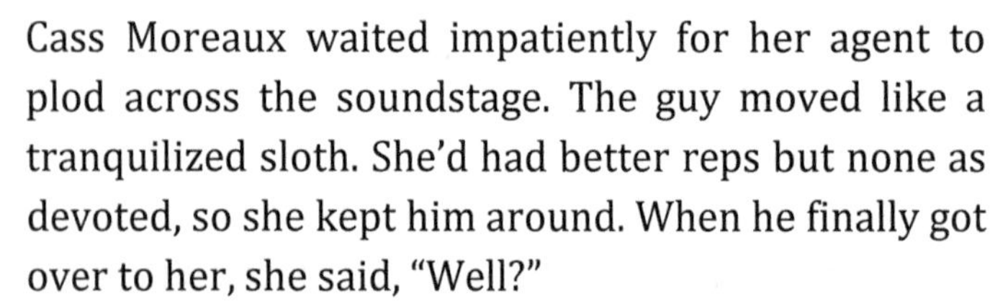

Cass Moreaux waited impatiently for her agent to plod across the soundstage. The guy moved like a tranquilized sloth. She'd had better reps but none as devoted, so she kept him around. When he finally got over to her, she said, "Well?"

He cleared his throat. "I'm sorry, Cass. The deal fell through. They won't do it."

"Good try, Freddie. I just got off the phone with Lenora Danmore. Besides, they take every drama queen who crawls out of rehab. And, by the way, you're not a very good actor," said Cass.

"Please, Cass. Just help me to understand. That's all I'm asking. There is no upside to this job. There is an immediate hit to your reputation and a high probability of complete disaster."

"Yeah, that pretty much sounds like *StarBash*," said Cass.

"And you know they own you, twenty-four hours a day for four months straight?"

"Yes," said Cass.

"And that's all you have to say?" He looked like a bully had just stolen his Popsicle.

"Uh...not exactly...I promised them some scandal."

"What?"

"It's no big deal. I'm a movie star. I specialize in that shit."

He didn't laugh.

"Come on, Freddie, it'll be fun. You can even help."

"I don't like it."

"You get to pick the scandal. Let's see...what's popular these days? OK, got it. Here are the options: casting-couch confessions, shoplifting at Nordstrom, mugshot from hell, or big-ass meltdown. Which one do you like?"

"None."

"Freddie. I'm going on that show. I don't expect you to like it—in fact, it means you're a pretty decent guy—but I'm going to do it. Now get your phone ready because you're about to record the biggest meltdown since Chernobyl."

Micah Bailey, a forty-three-year-old manager, producer, and newfangled game-show host, let his mind wander during yet another production meeting. He wondered what his life might have looked like if he had just walked away after getting fired for the very first time all those years ago. Would he be happy? Would he have been a good husband? Or would he be the same old dummy who had wasted his life trying to tame a ghost named Lenora?

And if one ghost isn't bad enough, why not open the door and welcome in another one? This ghost also had strong claws and a mean streak. Her name was *StarBash*, and like the other one, she had pounded stakes into Micah's life and showed no signs of ever leaving.

When the story broke, Hollywood had a big collective nervous breakdown. And Brandi Bonacore, who'd just turned in two weeks' notice at the diner, sat back and enjoyed the show. Cass Moreaux, the great Casmo, the big-time A-lister, had signed on for *StarBash* season four and, judging by the hand-wringing, it amounted to the worst kind of cataclysm...like Whole Foods running out of tofu. With a Budweiser in one hand, a mouse in the other, Brandi devoured blogs and websites like a caffeinated teenager. She especially liked the poison barbs in the comments sections: "That selfish bitch! This stunt will set honest actors back ten years!"; "If you need money, Cass, just drive to Porn Valley and shoot a few scenes with the polo team! At least you'd have some dignity left!"; "Slumming? This isn't slumming! Slumming looks like William Freakin' Shakespeare compared to this!"

Cass got an online ass-kicking for two weeks straight. Brandi slipped by mostly unscathed; the PC police had already knocked her out of the game, so nobody really cared if she crossed the line. She had nothing to lose and everything to gain—like a big movie deal. Not that she had any illusions about why Lenora Danmore had paid her the mysterious visit: *StarBash* needed someone to hurl shit at Cass Moreaux, and because of their past history, Brandi had gotten the job. No problem there. She'd let it fly. And she'd enjoy it. But when Brandi went to bed that night, she didn't only dream about destroying Cass Moreaux. She also dreamed about winning it all and finally getting her life back.

CHAPTER TWO

Micah stood on his spot two hundred feet in the air and held on to the weapon that hung across his chest. He almost liked the first show of the season because it had a live audience and gave him a chance to do some minor stunt work. The last show of the season ranked up there with the first because that's when everyone went home. In between it was just a job. And since they filmed on Lenora Danmore's estate, where he lived, sometimes it felt like a twenty-four-hour-a-day job.

He could have easily shut down *StarBash* after the first or second season. He owned the rights to the show—a condition he demanded before going into business with Lenora's production company—but now the thing had become a ratings monster dragging a slew of stakeholders along for a big fat money ride. It had become too big to kill. He closed his eyes and gathered his thoughts. No sense dwelling on these things now. Season four had been bought and paid for—no exchanges, no returns.

His earpiece crackled, and the director said, "Is Micah secured and ready?

"Secured and ready," said the stunt coordinator, who stood out of view just behind Micah.

The director continued, "OK, everyone, it's Wonka day. Take your places, stay on your game, and quiet on the set."

They called it Wonka day because on the first show of the season, they always had him make a big entrance like the guy in the movie.

The director and crew went through their routine:

"Sound?"

"Set."

"Cameras?"

"One set."

"Two set."

"Three set."

"Four set"

"Roll sound, roll cameras. Intro and light cue number one in five, four, three, two, go!"

Two massive searchlights penetrated the night and danced back and forth across the sky. The show's theme song enveloped the outdoor audience, five-thousand strong, and they eagerly clapped in time. "Ladies and gentlemen," boomed a man's voice from the mammoth speakers, "in 2017 we gave you Grand Central Station!" Applause. "In 2018 we gave you the RMS *Titanic*!" Loud applause. "Last year we gave you Alcatraz!" Louder applause. "And now, *StarBash 2020*, the highest-rated show in television history, is proud to present New York City's Plaza Hotel!" Mega kilowatts of lighting exploded onto the set and a giant curtain, four hundred feet by three hundred feet, fell dramatically to the ground to reveal what looked like an exact replica of the famed hotel. The theme song swelled majestically, and the audience erupted into applause.

Two powerful spotlights assaulted Micah's eyes. That was his cue. He stepped from the hotel's twentieth-floor fire escape onto a platform, pointed the flamethrower upward, and unleashed a geyser of fire into the night sky. The audience below roared.

A second later the audience got introduced to the first contestant by way of a videotaped bio projected from one of the hotel windows just a story below where Micah stood. The bio lasted twenty seconds and, as was normal for *StarBash*, the thirtysomething actress came across as a superficial dummy. Right before the video ended, Micah's specially rigged platform shot down to the window. He fired the flamethrower at the projected image. The actress sizzled, and the audience heard a loud, shrieking witch wail, like the one from *The Wizard of Oz*. Micah heard the audience laughter all the way up to the nineteenth floor.

The next videotaped bio began playing from a window on the next level down. This was contestant number two, a man who had always played the wholesome all-American type. Now the video showed him snorting cocaine a few decades past his heyday. He looked pudgy and decidedly unwholesome. After the video, just like before, Micah zoomed down, aimed the flamethrower, and sent the actor to hades. Another round of witch wail and laughter followed.

This is how the world met the actors on *StarBash 2020*: head shots that showed plastic surgery run amok; film clips of bad acting; viral videos of kinky sex, pathetic misdemeanors, desperate felonies, snobbery, tweets, retracted tweets, drugs, apologies, rehab, more drugs, more apologies, more rehab, and drunken escapades of every color. *StarBash* had a winning formula, and the world ate it up. And nobody knew how to serve it better than Micah Bailey.

"And now," boomed the announcer, "put your hands together to welcome your *StarBash* host, the Tinseltown terminator himself, Micah Bailey!"

Micah and his magic platform rocketed down to the stage like a George Jetson spaceship. It made a perfect two-point landing in front of the hotel. Micah dropped the flamethrower, thrust his fists into the air, and said, "Wow!"

The audience yelled, "Wow!"

"I said wow!" repeated Micah.

"I said wow!" exclaimed the audience.

Micah stepped off the platform and onto a strip of red tape that marked his spot. The platform disappeared back into the darkness and a lectern magically zoomed in from stage right and stopped right in front of him. Traditional comedy/tragedy masks adorned the lectern except the comedy figure had a bong attached to its mouth and tragedy wore a head scarf with a Gucci label. A large platform containing the actors, seated in two rows, briskly entered from stage left. They pretended to be relaxed. From behind his lectern, Micah faced the audience. The actors, some twenty feet from Micah, also faced the audience but at more of an angle.

Micah held up his hands and said, "It is now time to open these proceedings," the audience quieted. Micah continued, "I will ask you all to rise and for the gentlemen to remove your hats."

Everyone stood. The lights dimmed. The orchestra and choir added some religious flavor. Two spotlights, aimed at the sky, captured a black-and-white-marble pedestal as it slowly descended from the heavens. A shiny silver towel rack rested on the pedestal. A small purple towel, neatly folded, rested across the arm of the towel rack. The Greasy Dishrag had arrived.

"*StarBash 2020* has now officially begun!" exclaimed Micah.

The people in the audience responded like dyed-in-the-wool worshipers. Then everyone sat back down, and Micah continued his shtick, "Hello, ladies and gentlemen. Welcome to *StarBash 2020*, and welcome to the Plaza Hotel, New York, New York. You've gotten a close-up look at the hotel, and you've met our contestants. That means it's time to get down to business. Actors!" He yelled the word, and a few of them jumped in their seats. "On June 4, in exactly seventeen weeks, one of you is going to walk away with the Greasy Dishrag and a ten-million-dollar movie deal. To win that incredible prize, one of you is going to prove to the world that you are more than just an actor. You are going to prove that you are human. As in past seasons, you will start out at the top of society, where it's easy to fake your way through. And then, round by round, you will work your way down until you have been demoted to the very bottom, where only real people survive. Tonight you will dine in a luxurious penthouse. Four months from now, one of you will be scrubbing dishes in the kitchen. And that person will be the winner of the Greasy Dishrag!" The audience cheered, and the actors put on serious game faces, some more successfully than others.

Micah made eye contact with Cassandra Moreaux. If looks meant anything, she wanted to kill him. He winked at her. She mouthed an obscenity.

"Now," continued Micah, his voice quieter, "that's the good news. The bad news is there are fifteen of you and only ten will be checking in. That means"—his voice got louder—"it's time to play...paparazzi ping-pong!" The audience cheered as a giant game board descended stage right of Micah, angled so the actors could see it. A beautiful assistant named Tiffany Talador stood next to the board. Tiffany pointed at things. And since she belonged to the International Sisterhood of Pointers, Presenters, and Magicians' Assistants, one of Hollywood's most powerful unions, she got paid very well to do it. Micah gestured toward the board and said, "Here are your categories: 'Nanny Fanny,' 'Mother of All Tantrums,' 'Moving to Canada,' 'Do You Know Who I Am,' 'Mugshot Masterpiece,' 'Make Them Bigger,' and that good old standby, 'Addicted to Rehab.'" As Micah read the categories, Tiffany posed picturesquely and pointed at each one. "The game is simple," continued Micah, "you choose a category and name one of your fellow contestants who belongs in that category based upon recent paparazzi articles. If you choose correctly, your fellow actor is fired. If you choose incorrectly, you are fired. Now let's begin."

A shiny glass ping-pong-ball hopper shot up from under the stage. The balls bounced like popcorn in a popper. Micah pushed a button, and one of the balls released into a chute at the top. Micah took the ball and read the name, "Rye Steadly!" The audience clapped, and one of the actors pumped his fist, showcasing his impressive biceps in the process. Micah looked at the actor and said, "Rye, you seem happy. Why is that?"

The neatly coiffed forty-year-old flashed a smile that needed to be dimmed by half a megawatt and said, "I'm super stoked, Micah, 'cause let's just say the fruit is hanging low on this puppy. If I don't hit my head on it, I should be fine." The audience clapped on cue.

"OK, Rye," said Micah. "I guess we know what that means. Please choose your category."

"I'll take 'Mother of All Tantrums,'" said Rye.

A faint gasp and a murmuring of the word "Casmo" rippled through the audience. Micah pretended not to hear it. The actors craned their necks and looked at Cassandra Moreaux. She sat expressionless.

Micah smiled. He didn't trust her. She had no good reason to be on the show, and he didn't trust her. He continued, "OK, Rye, you've chosen 'Mother of All Tantrums.' According to the paparazzi, the actor listed in this category has thrown one or more viral tantrums that include all of the following: at least fifty cuss words, at least three broken objects, at least five minutes in length, and, finally, saying the words 'I am an artist' at least thirteen times. Rye Steadly, are you ready to name the 'Mother of All Tantrums'?"

"You betcha. I'm so ready."

"Who do you accuse?"

"I accuse Cassandra Moreaux!" said Rye, with a fist pump for a flourish.

The audience murmured loudly. Micah plowed forward. "Tiffany, please show us the answer."

Tiffany, the comely pointer, performed her magic, and a name instantly appeared. The audience gasped and, after a beat, clapped loudly. The displayed name was not Cassandra Moreaux. Rye Steadly slumped in his seat and looked sick. The chant of "Casmo" erupted spontaneously, first quietly then more loudly. Micah didn't understand. It was wrong...it was supposed to be...He looked at Cassandra Moreaux. She smiled and winked.

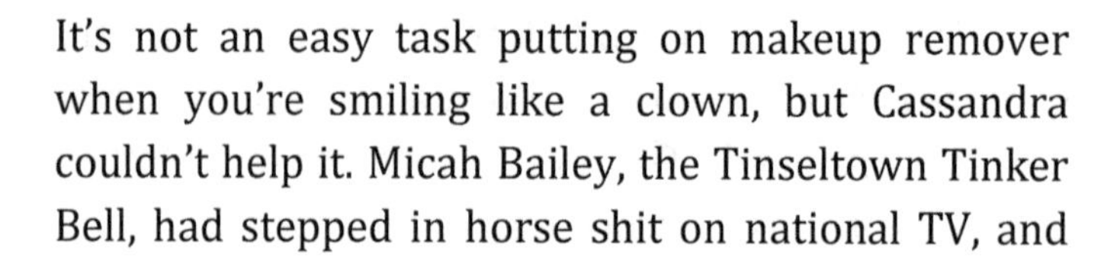

It's not an easy task putting on makeup remover when you're smiling like a clown, but Cassandra couldn't help it. Micah Bailey, the Tinseltown Tinker Bell, had stepped in horse shit on national TV, and she couldn't stop smiling. It almost made the whole dreadful experience worthwhile. Thank God the money guys were nothing if not predictable. That's how she knew she'd make it past the first round. For the last two weeks, they'd plastered her face on coast-to-coast commercials. They finally had a big name on their pathetic show, and they wanted to show it off; it didn't take a marketing wizard to know that they'd throw super-tubular Rye Steadly under the bus in a heartbeat if it meant keeping the golden goose safely locked up for another day.

And if that seemed crooked, nobody really cared. *StarBash* belonged on the lowbrow side of the performing-arts spectrum, next to roller derby and professional wrestling. So as long as the money guys got paid and the cretin audience got to see some movie star ass-slapping, everyone went home happy. Except Micah Bailey. Cass sat at the makeup table in her trailer and covered her cold-cream-slathered face with a warm washcloth.

Despite what Micah had exclaimed to the world, the actors lived full time in trailers on location, sequestered by contract from the rest of the world. The magnificent hotel with the penthouse suites had been movie magic made out of stage flats and scaffolding. Because of problems controlling the wind, the crew had assembled it that morning and broken it down that night. The rest of the shows were filmed on the soundstage or back lot, which contained smaller, more manageable portions of the façade. From façade to soundstage to back lot, the entire production took place on Lenora Danmore's estate, Rancho de Fresas, located eighty miles outside Los Angeles in the foothills northwest of Ventura. Lenora had purchased the property from one of the studios many years before and had spent her twilight years turning it into what was to be The Lenora Danmore Museum.

Cass turned out the light, slipped into bed, and closed her eyes. As her mind slowly wound down, backtracking over the events of the day, it got stuck in one particular spot, on a particular face, actually: Brandi Bonacore. She and Brandi shared an unpleasant history, and the sight of her sitting with the other contestants had unsettled Cass. *StarBash* loved putting microphones on troublemakers. And nobody in the world knew how to make trouble better than Brandi Bonacore—especially for Cass. This show had been a bad gamble in the first place. Cass didn't need a big-mouthed booby trap making it even worse. She thought about some different solutions to the problem, everything from bribery to a big diva tantrum, but eventually decided that maybe it didn't really matter. She had fulfilled her contractual commitment and had no intention of sticking with *StarBash* for more than a couple of episodes. During that time, she needed to concentrate on the real purpose: Lenora Danmore.

With any luck at all, she'd finish her business with Lenora the next morning. After that, Cass planned to orchestrate the fastest heave-ho departure in the history of reality TV. Goodbye *StarBash*, goodbye Lenora, goodbye Brandi-what's-your-name.

Lenora stepped into the doorway of the workshop. Micah stood across the room next to a sports car, his latest project. He ignored her. She admired his appearance, which had always been a secret source of pride for Lenora. He was handsome, not like a flashy European charmer but like one of those old-time salt-of-the-earth Americans who built log cabins and hunted wild game. He had simple, utilitarian, and neatly trimmed American good looks. Unfortunately, he also had the straight-and-narrow personality to go with it.

Lenora eased into the shop a few steps and said, "Micah..."

"Yes, Lenora." He compared paint samples to the hood of the car and didn't bother looking up.

"I've always...in my own way...been a dependable part of the team, haven't I?"

"OK," said Micah.

"And everyone knows 'dependable' is practically your middle name."

"What do you want, Lenora?"

Lenora told herself to stay calm. Micah had an infuriating way about him, especially when she wanted something. She continued: "We have always been a team."

"That's not why you're here," said Micah.

"The final two exhibits just came out of design."

"And…"

"They're calling for six more androids. We have to go for another season. I need the money. I need you to make the deal with the network," said Lenora.

"Disneyland opened with only twenty attractions and wet paint. Start with what you have and add to it as you go along," said Micah.

"This isn't Disneyland. It's more comparable to the theater, which means I'm only going to get one shot. If I don't make it on opening night, the museum is as good as dead. Why take that kind of risk when we don't have to?"

"I don't know what to tell you," said Micah. "I haven't made the deal because I haven't decided."

"You have the highest-rated show in history. What exactly is the problem?" said Lenora.

"We've become a mirror image of the institution that we're supposed to be mocking. That's the problem. We chase ratings and dollars, and we'll do anything to get them. And since we're talking about it, what happened out there with Cassandra Moreaux? We sacked the wrong actor, and we did it for the money."

"It's reality TV! What do you expect?" yelled Lenora.

"OK. I'll give you the answer. I haven't decided. That's the answer, and you're just going to have to live with it for now. There's plenty of time to worry about next season."

"I'm trying to be reasonable, Micah, but I'll drag you into court if I have to. You've seen me do it to others, and I'll do the same to you if I have to!"

"And tie up your money with high-priced lawyers? I don't think so."

"You listen to me, Micah! You make the deal, or we're through! Do you hear me? We're through!"

"Does that mean no more gin rummy?" asked Micah.

Lenora stormed out of the workshop. He'd done it to her again.

CHAPTER THREE

An hour before the scheduled meeting, Cass received a hand-delivered message from Lenora telling her that the meeting place had been changed. It said, "I'd like to show you my museum. Meet me inside. Just follow the signs. Pretend you're a tourist."

Cass cussed. She had done the show. She had lived up to her part of the bargain, and now she expected some good faith from Lenora. Instead she got manipulation.

Cass grabbed her handbag, closed the trailer door behind her, and did what the note said: She followed the signs—life-size images of Lenora—

that had been planted all over the property. There was Lenora the pauper flower girl, Lenora the gypsy with ruby-red lips and shiny dagger, Lenora the settler riding shotgun on a six-horse buckboard, etc. All of the signs pointed up the hill to a large Spanish-style structure, and all of them had the words "Lenora Danmore Museum." Farther on up, past the museum, sat Lenora's famous Victorian mansion. It looked like a predator hovering at the top of the mountain and could be seen from many miles around.

Cass looked down at her outfit. What do you wear to confront the woman who stabbed your mother in the back? Executioner garb might've been a little over the top, so she made do with a muted turquoise V-neck knit sweater with a gray scarf, gray skinny jeans, and simple flats. The outfit matched her mood...and the cold, gray February morning in California.

The signs, all positioned along a network of neatly trimmed converging paths, led to a cobblestone street that branched off from the main road that ran the length of the property. Cass followed the cobblestone street past a large parking lot until it ended at the Spanish tiled building. She stopped at a short distance for a look. A stucco archway spanned the cobblestone street. At the peak of the archway, an imposing sign, cast from solid bronze, said, "Lenora Danmore Museum." In front of the archway, two guard stations, with a striped boom gate between them, blocked the entrance to the museum. They'd obviously designed it to resemble the classic looks of an old-fashioned movie studio. Cass frowned. She'd seen her share of movie-star museums, and they usually left her feeling like she'd just witnessed an indecent display of self-gratification.

Cass approached one of the guard stations. It had a speaker and a ticket slot built into the glass. The portly guard on the other side of the glass smiled nd said, "Hello. Which call sheet are you reporting for?"

"Uh, excuse me?" said Cass.

The guard smiled again and massaged his double chin. And then he froze—catatonic, call-the-ambulance kind of froze—but before Cass had time to panic, a techno-digital voice said, "Please choose from one of these Lenora Danmore productions." And then the glass partition of the guard station lit up with a list of ten or fifteen of Lenora's movies.

"I'm here to see Lenora Danmore," said Cass.

Once again the digital voice said, "Please choose from one of these Lenora Danmore productions." Cass, not a Lenora Danmore fan to say the least, chose the least offensive movie from the list, and the guard instantly came back to life. She figured he must be some kind of android-robot thingy.

"Please type in your first name," he said.

Cass tapped out her name on a keyboard that appeared on the glass.

The guard smiled and said, "Thank you, Cass. Here's your pass. Please wear it around your neck, and keep it on at all times." He pushed a plastic card attached to a lanyard through the slot and said, "Now you better hurry, they're about to shoot your scene."

OK, that was bizarre...but kind of interesting, thought Cass. She stole another glance at the chubby robot and then passed through the raised boom gate and down the cobblestone street, which led to a large portico and a set of ornately carved wooden doors. Above the doorway a sign said, "Those Who Make Movie Magic Will Live Forever." The doors opened automatically and revealed a sight that caused Cass to stop dead in her tracks. She'd expected the usual claustrophobic shrine full of props, costumes, and a screening room that ran a never-ending loop of Lenora's first studio audition. And maybe a cheesy gift shop on the way out. What she actually saw was a chaotically busy studio courtyard full of rehearsing actors, harried craft workers, and a small army of manic gofers zigzagging every which way. A series of large rolling metal soundstage doors lined the sides of the courtyard. Each door had a big stencil number and a rotating beacon light next to it to indicate whenever filming might be taking place inside.

This is too much, thought Cass. *There's no way this is real.* She stepped forward for a closer look but immediately got intercepted by an electric cart. The driver of the cart—a perky twentysomething in a business skirt and a ponytail—said, "Hi. My name is Jo. Are you Cass?"

Cass didn't answer. She stared closely at the driver.

Then the driver repeated the question in exactly the same way with exactly the same voice inflection, and Cass became suspicious. She said, "Yes, I'm Cass. What's the circumference of the earth?"

"Twenty-four-thousand-nine-hundred-and-one miles."

"Who wrote *Symphony No. 9 in D Minor*?"

"Ludwig Van Beethoven."

"What is the official state dance of Wisconsin?"

"The state dance of Wisconsin is the polka."

Robot. The place is crawling with robots, thought Cass.

"It is nice talking with you, Cass. I am going to give you a lift to the soundstage. Please get into the cart, and place your hands on the black bar."

Cass climbed into the cart, and, just like at an amusement park, when she put her hands on the black bar, a different bar lowered onto her lap and locked her into place. She tried pulling up on the bar. It didn't budge an inch. The cart sped away.

"You are on stage nine, but I have to warn you, the director is in a bad mood. One of the performing dogs peed on his storyboard."

All right, that's it; this shit's getting scary, thought Cass, but before she had time to even think about it, the cart pulled into the soundstage. The restraining bar raised, and the driver said, "Here we are, Cass. Have a wonderful day, and remember...break a leg! Please exit to your right."

Cass got out of the cart and watched as it backed out into the courtyard. Then the big soundstage door closed and left her standing in the dark, except for a single beam of light that pointed to an escalator just a few feet away. Above the escalator entrance, an illuminated sign said, "Enter Here." The handrails of the escalator had embedded fluorescent lighting. She looked around the darkened stage and saw a glowing exit sign, an escape route, on the far wall. She thought about the two options for a second and then stepped on board the escalator; she needed the meeting with Lenora ASAP. When her foot hit the escalator tread, a voice said, "Please hold on to the handrails." The same message then repeated in Spanish, French, and Japanese.

As she moved forward into the mysterious darkness, Cass had the unpleasant realization that Lenora's museum project had started looking decidedly first class and that it actually had her halfway hooked.

The escalator passed through a small opening in a black curtain and into a wide-open soundstage where up ahead Cass saw an exact recreation of the barn interior from *Simon's Glory*, one of Lenora's early movies. But, she realized as she got closer, the set didn't just depict the interior of the barn; it depicted the whole shoot: director, cameraman, camera assistant, sound crew, light crew, barn animals. It looked immaculate, perfect in every detail, and even though it showed only a static display, it looked ready to jump right onto the movie screen. She stared...maybe more than halfway hooked.

The escalator voice dislodged Cass from her gaze. It said, "Please prepare to disembark," delivered in English and subsequent languages. At the end of the line Cass stumbled forward into a partitioned viewing section. The large barn scene occupied one side of the exhibit, and the viewing section, where she now stood, occupied the other.

"Hello, my dear."

The voice startled Cass. She turned, expecting another robot encounter but saw Lenora. There was no mistaking the high cheekbones accented by green eyes. Everything else didn't look quite as recognizable. The refined nose had plumped somewhat with age, and the perfect lines of her famous face had given way to some droop and jowl. For an eighty-seven-year-old, she still looked pretty good, though. Cass fumbled for some words and said, "Lenora Danmore..."

"Yes, and you're Cassandra Moreaux. Come closer, and let me look at you."

Cass stepped closer.

"And there's that beautiful blonde hair, one color but so many shades. You can't buy hair like that. The same goes for your elegant neckline. You can ruin it by eating too many potatoes, but you can't buy it. Now teeth, those you can buy, and you obviously did, but that's OK. Overall, you still have a great deal of your original equipment. Do yourself a favor, and keep it that way because plastic surgery is like a French cookbook; the pictures look beautiful, but in real life the results are sometimes scary. There, that will be the last of the unsolicited advice. Now, tell me what you think of my little project."

This lady is sharp, thought Cass, *maybe a little too sharp, but it beats a drooling bib and diapers.* She answered the question, "What do I think? Unexpectedly surprised, I guess you could say."

"'Unexpectedly surprised' is probably OK, considering you haven't even seen the best part yet. It's interactive. You have to experience it to get the full effect. Go stand in that circle, and you'll see what I mean. I'll sit over here and watch," said Lenora, as she pointed toward the display.

Cass didn't like the way Lenora had quickly taken control of the conversation, but before Cass had a chance to say anything, Lenora had turned her back. Cass watched as she walked to one of the cushioned benches that lined the back wall. She wore a green sleeveless China print dress and had good posture and a strong gait. She didn't look anything close to her age. *Whatever she is on, I want some of it*, thought Cass.

Cass turned toward the display and noticed a peninsula walkway that jutted out from the rest of the partition. At the end of the protrusion, in the heart of the set, was an illuminated circle. It still had a handrail partition, but it occupied a space in the middle of all the action. She walked up to it. Inside the illuminated circle, fluorescent green words rhythmically flashed on and off. They said, "You have talent! Step inside, and show the world!"

She stepped into the circle, and the static display instantly exploded into life. The crew started moving, talking, and working. Two goats played together, rearing up and banging their heads. Two stalled horses chewed hay and stared at the film crew.

Cass stepped out of the circle and, after a delay of two or three seconds, everything powered down. She looked over at Lenora, who had a pleased look on her face. "How is this even possible?" asked Cass.

"It's the card you're wearing around your neck. You are instantly recognized by every cast member in every exhibit. Now keep going; it gets even better," said Lenora.

Cass stepped back into the illuminated circle, and the scene sprang back to life. The director, who'd previously been frozen with his eye up to the camera, walked straight up to Cass and said, "Now remember, Cass, Simon's Glory has just been taken in the claiming race, and Sarah doesn't know it. All she knows is that he won the race, and she's happy. Are you ready?"

"Uh...yes," said Cass.

The director stepped back and said, "Sound, camera, marker."

A camera assistant popped in front of the camera with his clapperboard and said, "Scene one, take one."

"And...action," said the director.

Cass heard a voice hollering, "Maggie! Maggie! Maggie!" A girl charged hard through the open barn door. She suddenly put on the brakes and happily slid for ten feet on the slippery plank floor.

It was Lenora! An exact android replica of Lenora, as she had played the role of Sarah Simon back in 1954, now stood just a few feet from Cass. That slide into the barn had become an icon of American movie history—even if Cass had never been impressed by it.

"What do you say now, Maggie? Is Simon still a cart horse?" said Sarah.

"Uh…no…Sarah…Simon's not a…cart horse," stumbled Cass. Then she saw her lines projected on the wall, and she continued, "He's a…champion. And you…uh…knew it—"

"Stop, stop. Keep rolling," said the director. "Cass, what's going on? You sound like you're counting pickles in a pickle factory."

"I know, I know, sorry," said Cass.

"OK, take it from 'No, Sarah.' And…action," said the director.

"No, Sarah. Simon's not a cart horse. He's a champion. And you knew it from the beginning. When we gave up, you still believed in him. He's everything you believed, Sarah. Everything. And I want you to always remember it, because you're the one who made it possible."

"And cut! That's the way, Cass. Beautiful. Print it," said the director.

Young Lenora walked up to Cass and said, "Good job, Cass. Keep up the good work. And do not forget to pick up a copy of our scene from the gift store. I think you will like it."

"Thank you, Miss Danmore; I appreciate it," said Cass.

Young Lenora left the barn the same way she'd entered, and the crew went back to their original positions. That's when Cass came to her senses and wondered what the hell had just happened. They were robots! She'd just apologized to a robot director and groveled before a robot actor. She didn't do that to real humans! She stepped outside the circle. After a few seconds the robots powered down. Cass looked at Lenora. She was smiling more than ever. *All right, time to regroup. This isn't how the meeting is supposed to be going*, thought Cass.

"Your professional instincts kicked in. I saw it," said Lenora when Cass joined her on the bench. Lenora took one of Cass's hands and continued: "I'm sorry, dear; I should have warned you that I added this little experiment to our meeting. We've tested on hundreds of regular people but not once on an actor. I'm very pleased with the results."

"I'm happy it turned out that way because I need your help, as well," said Cass, in a businesslike way.

"Yes, I know you do. I can't make any guarantees, but we did make a deal, so here we are," said Lenora, giving Cass's hand a little squeeze before letting go.

"And I'm glad we're finally here, Lenora. I almost started thinking that you might be trying to avoid me," said Cass.

"Oh heavens, dear. I wish my life had that much drama. Unfortunately, it's just old age. I don't get around like I used to, and all correspondence is handled by Micah."

Ah, Micah Bailey, the rodent with perfect hair. Cass had some pointed questions on that topic, but she didn't dare waste her opportunity. Instead, she pressed forward: "I need to ask you about my mother, Wendy Rainy."

"That's what I assumed, but we need to be very clear about something, Cassandra. I agreed to a meeting, but that doesn't mean I'll talk about everything under the sun. That business happened seventy years ago, and with my failing memory, it would be too easy to misremember and cause serious damage, not just to myself but to others as well. Besides, the whole sad saga has been covered from a dozen different angles, and nothing has ever changed."

"Maybe that's because everyone has focused on the wrong thing," said Cass.

"And what does that mean?"

"They focused on what can be seen instead of what's missing," said Cass, as she retrieved a paper from her handbag. She held it up and said, "This is a copy of the letter addressed to Wendy Rainy from the Chicago Communist Party. It was the evidence used against her—"

"I know what it is. What's your point?"

"We know this was given to the FBI by one of her roommates, but we don't know which one. We also know she had only three roommates from the time she moved to Hollywood: you and two others. And that's what's missing: your file. Why does the FBI have files on the other two roommates but not on you?"

"Because I'm not a communist."

"And neither were they."

"Then I don't know. Maybe you should ask the FBI," said Lenora.

"I did," said Cass, "through the Freedom of Information Act, and I got nothing."

"So now, based upon nothing but your imagination, you've embarked on the grand crusade," said Lenora. "I have to ask myself: Why? What arrogance would compel you to disturb other people's lives in such a manner?"

"It's not other people, Lenora. It's me, my life. I lived under the weight of that blacklist almost as much as my mother. And I still do. That's what happens when you grow up with a broken mother. It never leaves you."

"I'm sorry for that," said Lenora, "just as I'm sorry for anyone who suffers, but your whole mistaken premise seems to be that since you can't find a certain file—that never existed in the first place—then I must be guilty of something."

"You're leaving out the important part," said Cass. "My mother had been cast as Ruby in *Monty's Revenge*. After she got blacklisted, the part went to you. You were the only one who benefited."

"That's a lie that has been refuted in court."

"Not exactly," said Cass. "It never made it to court because you paid off your accusers, and they changed their stories."

Lenora stared sadly into Cass's eyes for a moment and then said, "You and I are connected in so many ways, Cassandra, including a relationship with your wonderful mother. I very much wanted this meeting to go well, and it saddens me to have to tell you that if you persist in this witch hunt, it will end in regret and attorney fees, and all of it will be on you. I won't have any other choice."

"Actually, I'm glad you brought that up, Lenora, because there is an easier way to settle it; just give me a copy of your birth certificate," said Cass.

When Lenora heard the words "birth certificate," her face flushed white, and a tiny muscle in her cheek began twitching. If this had happened on set, she no doubt would have demanded a reshoot. She couldn't do that now. Cass continued: "You see, Lenora, I searched every name associated with my mother's case, including your birth name, Carolyn Anna Voyt. When everything came back blank, I hired a detective to chase down the Voyt family from Milwaukee, Wisconsin. He had no trouble finding them, and it turns out that Adam and Monica did indeed have a daughter named Carolyn. But she wasn't a famous actress. She was a bookkeeper in a sausage factory. She died in 1998. I'm sure you can see how all this makes me wonder what you might be hiding."

"I'm not hiding anything," said Lenora. "My birth name is Carolyn Voyt. You can send your detective back to Milwaukee, and he'll find school records and photographs and medical records that all belong to me. I can't help it if some lady in a sausage factory happens to have the same name. How do you know they sent the correct birth certificate? Voyt is a very common name in Milwaukee."

"Like I said, there's a simple way to settle it. Just give me a copy of the one you have, and I'll try again."

Cass had her. She saw it in the involuntary darting of the eyes as Lenora searched in vain for an escape. Cass continued: "In case you don't know, Lenora, I can turn all this over to the Internet, and I'll have an answer in twenty-four hours. A picture of the bogus certificate, a tempting reward, and ten million Internet junkies will go to work. I almost did it when I couldn't arrange a meeting. But now here we are. We might as well do it right."

Lenora remained silent for a moment and then said, "What happens after you do your search and find nothing?"

"Then I move on, still looking, but not looking at you."

"And would you be willing to tell the media that I've been exonerated?"

"Yes, I would," said Cass.

"And we will be friends once again?"

This last turn in the conversation surprised Cass, but, then again, maybe it didn't. Lenora had the strong personality of someone who had climbed to the very top of Hollywood. For her the idea of running up the white flag might take a little while longer to sink in. For now Cass didn't mind playing along. She answered the question: "Yes, friends once again."

"Then I'll do it. I'll break my rule and do it. But it's going to take a few weeks...because...it's...uh...coming from a foreign country."

The two ladies shared tepid smiles before Lenora said, "Now that we have that unfortunate business behind us, perhaps you will be willing to step into the circle and test one more scene for me? The grand opening is just a few months away, and we're terribly behind schedule."

"I think I can do that," said Cass. She stood and walked toward the circle.

"Cassandra," said Lenora.

Cass turned back. "Yes, Lenora."

"Just for curiosity sake, what are your intentions...if you ever find the person you're looking for?"

Cass smiled genuinely and said, "To destroy their life like they destroyed my mother's. And it doesn't matter if they are dead or alive. I'll ruin them forever." And then she stepped into the circle, and the set came back to life, just as before, except now Sarah Simon (Lenora the robot), who had entered the barn, looked to be seventeen or eighteen years old and fully grown.

"OK, girls," said the robot director. "Sarah has just found out about Maggie's engagement to Byron Snedeger, and she is deeply hurt and not thinking clearly. Are you ready?"

"Sure, let's do it," said Cass.

"Sound, camera, marker."

"Scene two, take one."

"And...action!"

Sarah stood about fifteen feet away and clutched a blue wildflower in one hand, held out slightly in front of her body. She stared intently at Cass. She started to approach, in a creeping, funereal kind of way. She didn't smile or blink. Cass struggled to remember the scene, without success. She looked for her lines projected on the wall, like before, but found none. Sarah continued to approach until the two stood face to face just inches apart.

"This is for you, Maggie...to remember the way things used to be," said Sarah. She handed the wildflower to Cass and continued: "And this is for the way things are now." Sarah raised her right hand and slapped Cass across the face. The violent force of the blow threw Cass out of the circle and planted her facedown on the floor. Cass moaned and rubbed her cheek. The robots powered down. After a few seconds, she propped herself up on an elbow. She wiped the tears from her eyes and saw two legs standing before her. They belonged to Lenora.

"Oh my. I guess we have a small glitch," said Lenora.

Cass looked up in time to see a thin smile pass from Lenora's wrinkled lips. Cass then sat up the rest of the way and said, "I like your museum, Lenora, but you might want to think about the part where the customer gets bitch-slapped by the robot."

CHAPTER FOUR

Brandi turned the corner on her way back from wardrobe and saw a black limousine parked next to her trailer. It hadn't been there earlier in the day. She didn't like it. Powerful people rode in limousines, and, in her experience, they didn't mind throwing that power around.

She pretended to ignore the car and made a show of fussing for her trailer key. But then the uniformed driver got out of the car and opened the back door. He said, "Please get in, Miss Bonacore."

Get in, my ass, thought Brandi. She stopped ten feet short of the car and looked inside. Lenora

Danmore sat in one of the backseats. She looked mad. Without saying a word, she pointed at an empty seat, and Brandi obediently climbed in. The driver closed the door.

The two ladies sat facing each other. Lenora just stared.

"To the club, Charles," said Brandi, in a bad English accent.

Lenora didn't crack a smile. Brandi thought about telling a dirty joke. Lenora held out a small cream-colored envelope. Brandi took the envelope and said, "What is it?"

"It's the answers to this week's competition, so I guess you can call it a free pass. And there will be more for the following shows. In fact, I expect that you are going to have a very profitable relationship with StarBash Productions."

"Yeah, and what do I gotta do for you?" asked Brandi.

"You don't have a high regard for the etiquette of deal making, do you, Miss Bonacore?"

"Since I don't know what you're talking about, I'd say probably not."

"All right. Here's what I expect," said Lenora. "You will have a long run on the show, and you will win more than your fair share of the contests. In return you will not fire Cassandra Moreaux. You will keep her on the show."

"Forever?"

"Until I say otherwise."

Brandi agreed, and the meeting ended. But as soon as she got into her trailer, she tore the cheat sheet into a hundred little pieces. She wanted to win. She wanted it badly. But not like that.

Micah attached the air hose to the orbital sander and studied the security monitors. They showed two of his security guards escorting Cassandra Moreaux to his workshop. He had a regular office upstairs next to Lenora's but didn't like it. It contained too much persnickety technology—computers, printers, routers, apps, boots, reboots, bugs, crashes—and not enough power tools. So, after construction on the museum finished, he moved everything down to the new workshop, and that kind of evened things out. Lenora threw a fit, but he didn't mind. She needed a steady supply of monkey wrenches to keep her in check.

His eyes swept over the workshop and noticed the picture of his wife on his desk. Actually it was his ex-wife. He quickly went over and put the picture in one of the desk drawers. He didn't like explaining it to strangers—mostly because he couldn't even explain it to himself. He glanced again at the security monitors. Everything looked good. Professional. His guards had their fawning under control, and

Princess Cassandra didn't seem to be throwing a tantrum. They still had a few hundred yards to go, so he returned to the sander and turned the buzzing device loose on the hood of the car.

The picture changed a few minutes later when the threesome skipped into the shop like they'd just been frolicking on the yellow brick road. One look at the star-struck faces said it all; his normally lethargic guards looked exuberant. Micah found it embarrassing. And aggravating. If these same two guys met someone who actually deserved their attention, like a scientist or an inventor, they'd nod their heads and go sneak a nap in the break room.

"Micah, Micah, take a picture of me and Casmo. My wife's gonna die!" said Manny.

"Yeah, yeah, me too, Micah," said Jabril.

"Hold on, boys," said Cassandra, "One at a time. You first, Manny, but first you have to tell me, is your wife the jealous type?"

"Uh...yeah, she kinda is."

"OK, then let's just do a side-by-side with a big smile for the camera. Are you ready, Mr. Cameraman?" said Cass.

She liked barking out orders. *What a surprise,* thought Micah. He took a phone from his pocket and snapped the picture.

"Now what about your wife, Jabril? Is she jealous?" asked Cassandra.

"Nah, not her. She thinks I'm too ugly to worry about," said Jabril.

"Really. Maybe we should give her something to think about. Let's do a friendly cheek-to-cheek smile for the camera," said Cass.

The giddy guard and the big movie star embraced, and Micah took the picture.

"Uh...I just remembered...my wife's not jealous either. Can I get another one?" said Manny.

"Really, Manny? All right, this can be your secret one," said Cassandra.

After another pose and another ridiculous picture, Micah put away the phone and said, "That's it, guys; the photo shoot is over. Time to get back to work."

"What about you, Micah? Don't you want one?" asked Manny.

Unfortunately, before Micah had the pleasure of answering that absurd question, Jabril said, "You idiot. They're on the show together. Why would he want a picture when he's got that?"

"I don't know," said Manny, as he and Jabril started to leave. "Maybe he doesn't have enough memory on his phone for the show, so maybe he wants a picture instead."

"You're an idiot."

"And you're ugly...just like your wife says."

"That was quite a show you put on," said Micah, after the guys had left. "I'm impressed."

"Don't be. You could be dying of boredom, and I wouldn't put on a show for you. Now why am I here?" said Cassandra.

"That's what I want to know. Why are you here?" said Micah.

"You mean *StarBash*?" asked Cass.

Micah nodded.

"I'm here because I'm a pissed-off actor who's tired of watching some reality-star goon attack our reputation on national TV. You wanna know why I'm here? I'll tell you. I'm here because you've turned meanness and hatred into a blood sport, and I'm going to beat you at your own game!"

Talk about a canned speech. Micah didn't believe a word of it. He grabbed a small stack of letters off the workbench, held them up for Cass to see, and said, "Let me help you out a little bit. You sent four letters and ten emails asking for a meeting with Lenora. She declined. The next thing I know, you're on *StarBash*, and you're having a meeting with Lenora."

"How do you know I had a meeting with Lenora?" asked Cass.

"It's my job," said Micah. "I get paid to stay one step ahead. Now, do you care to revise your monologue? And I should probably warn you that the angry-drama-queen thing doesn't work with me. You have to remember who I work for. I'm immune to it."

"OK, fine," said Cass. "You're immune to drama queens, and I'm immune to pompous assholes. I guess we won't be having any sleepovers. What a shame." She tossed out a fake smile and started looking around the workshop.

That was good, thought Micah. He was a pompous asshole...but only with actors. Pompous asshole versus pretentious movie star. What could be more fun? He eyed Cassandra as she looked at some photographs on the wall by his desk. This was the first time he'd seen her up close without bright stage lighting, and it surprised him. She wore minimal makeup, if any at all, and she looked normal, which was saying something for a Hollywood actor pushing thirty-five. The mere fact that her lips hadn't been Botoxed into a couple of pouting bratwursts was a miracle in itself. She had a friendly, natural smile and innocent hazel eyes. And either she hadn't been raised in sunny California, or her mother had locked her in a closet because she still had smooth, youthful skin. He'd seen her face in magazines for makeup ads. She looked good, but he liked this natural version better. Even her blonde hair, with long body curls, steered more toward the natural side. All in all, Micah could see how Hollywood, in its deep shallowness, had made such a big deal over such a package.

"I recognize these," said Cass, motioning to the pictures. "That's from *Operation Scorpion,* this is

Irish Lullaby, and this is *Mobster and the Maid*. Who's the kid?"

Micah didn't answer. She looked at him, looked at the pictures, looked back at him and said, "All right, this really screws things up. You're the big actor-basher, but here you are—what, six, seven years old?—hanging with the actors."

Micah shrugged and said, "I had a relative who worked at the studio."

"Sorry, that doesn't make any sense. These movies are from different studios. Do you care to revise your monologue, Mr. Drama Queen?"

Micah tried not to smile.

"What's that?" she asked, pointing at the car Micah had been working on.

"A 1956 Ford Thunderbird. It's being restored," said Micah.

"And then what? Are you going to cruise Main Street and maybe hang out at the malt shop?"

"Then it goes in here," said Micah. He walked to the far end of the shop and opened a set of double doors.

She followed him through the doorway and said, "Whoa."

Micah liked that response better than her usual sarcasm. "Do you like cars?" he asked.

"Not particularly, but I like shiny things. What is it?"

"It's part of the museum," said Micah, looking over a giant showroom of cars. "They're famous cars from famous movies. Lenora added it mostly for the husbands...and anyone else who might like cars better—" A loud shriek interrupted him. He watched Cassandra dash over to a burned-out Chrysler.

"Oh my gosh! I love this car!" she said, as Micah caught up with her.

"'Do you feel this vehicle is safe for highway travel?'" said Cassandra in a deep voice. She then changed her facial expression and said, "'Yes, officer, I do. I really do,'" And then she burst out laughing.

Micah watched.

"Come on! It's from *Planes, Trains & Automobiles*, one of my all-time favorites!"

Micah said nothing.

"All right, you know what? You really know how to kill the moment."

"I don't go to movies."

Cass stared blankly and then said, "How come I'm not surprised? What about Lenora's movies?"

"Especially not hers," said Micah.

"I don't know...it sounds like you've got a passive-aggressive thing going on there. You might want to deal with it before it gets worse." She delivered a smart-ass smile and then said, "Goodbye, Micah Bailey, the terminator from Timbuktu."

"You still haven't answered my question," said Micah. "Why are you here?"

"Because I love reality TV. What else could it be? Now I have a question for you. Why do you hate actors?"

"Because the actor promised the ring around the collar would disappear, and it didn't. What else could it be?"

"Goodbye, Micah."

She turned and left. Micah called out after her, "I will find out why you're here, Cassandra. You can count on it. And if you have any more meetings with Lenora, I need to know about them in advance."

"And why is that?" she yelled, over her shoulder.

"Let's just say it's better that way."

She didn't respond.

The day after Cass's meeting with Lenora, she found a small envelope that had been slipped under the door of her trailer. For the briefest moment she thought that maybe Lenora had given up the charade and had coughed up the birth certificate. She had to know that her act hadn't fooled anyone. First, she practically fainted when Cass mentioned the birth certificate, and the private detective, and the phony family in Milwaukee. Secondly, super meticulous Lenora Danmore claimed not to have a copy of her very own birth certificate. And, thirdly, she immediately started stalling with some story about getting the certificate from a foreign country. The lady was guilty as hell, but Cass had done the right thing; she'd given her a chance to tell the truth. She didn't deserve even that much. Now, while Lenora pretended to wait on slow mail from Siberia, Cass already knew her next move, and it didn't require her to stay with *StarBash* one minute longer. Mission accomplished.

The envelope under the door turned out to be a duplicitous note from Lenora that said:

Dear Cassandra,

Every friendship has issues. That is just one of the joys of being human. I have no doubt that in time our friendship will be stronger than ever. To that end, if you have any other questions, I'm happy to meet with you at any time.

Kindest regards,
Lenora

Forget it, lady, thought Cass. Your robot already decked me once. I'm not going anywhere near you.

It had certainly been a strange few days at Rancho de Fresas. First Cass had played cat and mouse with Lenora, and then she played a loopy game of screwball with Micah, Lenora's forty-year-old babysitter. What a bizarre combination: Lenora Danmore, the ruthless, scheming maniac, and Micah

Bailey, the actors' manager who hated actors. That was pretty messed up, even by Hollywood standards.

The story about how the two got together was also quite bizarre and actually something of a legend in the business. The most common version of the story said that by the mid-nineties Lenora's career had stalled due to a reputation for temper tantrums that led to cost overruns on every project she worked on. Besides the directors and producers who'd stopped taking her calls, she'd also lost favor with the best agents and managers; either they knew her and didn't want the grief, or they were newbies who abandoned ship after the first storm. Enter Micah Bailey, who couldn't have been more than twenty years old. He took the job and drove straight to Beverly Hills to see Fred Suggerman, who at the time happened to be casting the female lead for *Melancholy Murder*. According to the legend, Micah smoothed Fred over with a bunch of double-talk about some special technique for Lenora that worked every time, and Fred gave the part to Lenora, presumably just to see how the whole thing played out, more than anything else.

And, whether this account is to be believed or not, Micah really did have a special technique, and it actually worked quite well. Whenever Lenora got out of control, Micah dove right in and took the fight to her. This meant that when she crossed the line, she always had a war on two fronts waiting for her: the producer and Micah or the director and Micah or the costume designer and Micah, etc. Of course, Lenora didn't put up with mouthy subordinates, so she'd go after Micah and shred him from top to bottom. Then she'd fire him. By this point in the ordeal, more times than not, Lenora's spleen would be mostly drained, and she'd be inclined to listen to reason. But the real beauty of it all, whether by plan or not, was that Micah never stayed fired. Lenora fired the hell out of him one day, and he showed up the next day like nothing had ever happened. Micah ended up making a great living by being the most fired employee in the world.

Where did the facts of this story end and the embellishment begin? Nobody cared. Hollywood likes stories with some swagger. But it probably contained elements of both. On one hand, nobody doubted Lenora's shrewdness. You don't reach the top of the Hollywood heap without it. She saw that her career had faltered, so she took action. She didn't need to concoct a scheme with a teenager. On the other hand, it was a fact that Micah took no shit from Lenora. He did what it took to keep her moving forward, and that included toe-to-toe combat that had been witnessed dozens of times all over town. And he did get fired over and over again. It was a bizarre arrangement but the bottom line was that Lenora added ten years to her career and did some of her best work. And Micah, even now, fifteen years later, had the reputation of a miracle worker. Any number of the best producers and directors, especially the older ones, would gladly take his call, and the offensiveness of *StarBash* didn't faze them at all.

For Cass personally, the guy came off as more of a handsome simpleton than a miracle worker. He had simple clothes, a simple short haircut, and a ninety-nine-word vocabulary. She'd cast him as the dumb potato farmer any day of the week. He looked like the kind of guy who could go to a party, not say twenty words, and have a wonderful time. He looked like the kind of guy who flossed daily and checked the air in his tires once a week. He looked annoyingly punctual. He was the exact opposite of any man Cass had ever been involved with...which probably wasn't saying very much.

And that pretty much summed up Cass's first week at the ranch. Except...since she had been the fortunate witness of all this free weirdness, she must have felt compelled to add some of her own because she had an exceptionally weird dream about her ex-husband during this same time. In the dream he kneeled piously, decked out like Sir Lancelot, as the pope prepared to bestow a medal on him. The ceremony took place in a giant cathedral, where Cass sat in the audience. Just before the pope placed the medal around his neck, Cass stood up and interrupted the ceremony with a poem:

Oh so many important things to say
But who will listen to your speech today
He's a dandy man who's fond of many words

Fold your humble hands and let the words flow
Nobody cares that you really don't know
He's a dandy man who's fond of many words

Fancy speeches always seem to make sense
Until the dirty dog jumps the back fence
He's a dandy man who's fond of many words

Then two medieval guards escorted Cass to the dungeon to be tortured.

Lenora and Micah lived in the hundred-year-old Victorian on top of the hill. They each had private living quarters on the second floor. Micah's wife, Heather, had also lived there when the two had been married. The honor and prestige of sharing a mansion with a living legend had sounded like a dream come true to Heather. And Micah bought into her excitement even though he should have known better. Now he lived alone in two thousand square feet, and it felt like an airplane hangar. Thankfully, the staff of eight added enough humanity to the house to make it habitable. He also sometimes enjoyed sitting in on the weekly get-togethers Lenora hosted for her old actor friends—except when the get-togethers turned into drunken fan-club meetings for her highness. All of these friends had enjoyed some success in Hollywood, but that success had stopped putting food on the table decades ago. They faithfully played Lenora's party games, careful not to ever outshine their hostess, and then they devoured enough food and drink to hold them over until the next get-together.

Micah had started a private tradition in the house many years earlier: he took on the nightly job of serving Lenora her nightcap. At first he had done it because of an imaginary bond between the two of them that he thought deserved some special attention. Later, when he figured out that his bond with Lenora had never existed, he did it for business reasons; Lenora was a moving target who didn't have the best communication skills, so Micah used the time to talk business or get answers to questions. Nowadays he served the nightcap out of habit, like most things in his life.

On this night, however, Micah actually had a question on his mind as he took Lenora her drink that contained two ounces of cherry juice, half a shot of bourbon, and a twist of lemon—a recipe that never changed under pain of death. He knocked on the door. She said, "Put it on the coffee table."

Micah entered the reception area that separated the office from the bedroom. He put the tray on the table and poked his head into the office doorway. Lenora sat at the desk and had her eyes locked onto a computer monitor that showed the latest exhibit set designs. Micah said, "Lenora?"

"What?"

"How, exactly, did you convince Cass Moreaux to go on the show?" asked Micah.

Lenora's head slumped, and she sighed, just loud enough for Micah to hear. She removed her reading glasses, swiveled around, and said, "Has she said something to you?"

"No."

"Then why worry about it? She's ratings gold. That's all that matters."

"You're pulling strings behind my back, and I don't like it. Does it have anything to do with Wendy Rainy?" asked Micah.

Lenora hated getting cornered. She glared for a second and then said, "She wanted me to answer questions about her mother, and I wanted her on the show. So we made a deal. You should be thanking me, unless an extra million is too much of a burden for you."

"And will you be having any more meetings?" asked Micah.

"I hope so. Imagine what she could do for the museum—not that it's any of your business."

"She's on the show, so it's my business, and I keep track of my business."

"Good. Keep track of your business, and keep your nose out of mine," said Lenora.

Micah turned around. On his way out he said, "Good night, Lenora. See you in the morning."

She didn't answer.

CHAPTER FIVE

"And here's your *StarBash* host, the Tinseltown terminator himself, Micah Bailey!"

"Hello, America! Welcome to *StarBash 2020*, and welcome to the grand ballroom of the Plaza Hotel!" said Micah, like an infomercial hawker.

Cass watched as her fellow contestants, with whom she had been grouped, ardently fawned over Micah Bailey. They clapped and smiled and nudged one another aside so that they might be seen by his highness. Cass didn't bother. Micah stood nearby and filmed his opening monologue, the format of which never changed: insult Hollywood, belittle the actors, and reveal the challenge that will get one of them fired from the show.

He said, "Wow! Congratulations to each of you. You've made it to the top. You are living large at the Plaza Hotel. You slumber in a bed of the finest linen, sometimes with your spouse, sometimes with the nanny. Your morning Bloody Mary is served on a silver platter. You prepare for the rigors of the day with a massage and a manicure. Your million-dollar face is coated with the finest Corinthian mud. Be careful now; don't get any of that stuff under your fingernails. And then you are ready. More than ready. You are important. You are powerful. You take power lunches and make power deals. You power through the day trailing a glittery blanket of powerfulness. And after you've unleashed all the power that is humanly possible, cocktail hour arrives just in the nick of time. And, my friend, with your Wang or your Armani and your surgically sculpted boozy glow, it can truthfully be said that nobody does cocktail hour better than you.

"Oh my, it has certainly been a busy day, but, alas, there's no rest for the adored because now it's time to retire to dinner, where you will cast aside the menu and tell the chef exactly how to cook the meal, right down to the last sautéed truffle. And then it's off to the televised awards ceremony. It's the third one this week, but that's OK because actors just love it when the world watches them pat one another on the back. You pose and smile and clap on cue. And, cross your fingers, if your name is called, you will boldly mount the soapbox and turn the American people into your personal political prisoners. When the speech ends, your enlightened peers will rise to their feet in admiration. And then the celebration continues at the after-party, where you will pontificate about tolerance and the importance of respecting opinions. Unfortunately, the only difference of opinion at this party will be about which Westside bistro serves the best veggie burger. And now, at last, it's time to return to your suite and bring the day to a close. You apply a generous portion of the Essential Essence of Essentialness to your face and put cucumbers on your eyes. Then you turn out the light. Oh, what a day! What a marvelous movie-star day!"

And how did Cass's proud colleagues respond to this twisted diatribe? They smiled for the cameras and clapped. Cass stood in their midst, in the middle of a dumb flock of free-range fryers, and watched as they celebrated the man who had just butchered their self-respect. But then she realized that it made perfect sense; they had sold their souls when they signed up for the show. Let Micah say what he wanted. They cared about the money and nothing else.

The cameras kept rolling, and Micah kept talking, "And now, dear beautiful people of Hollywood, tonight nine of you will move one step closer to your ten-million-dollar movie deal!"

More applause from the flock.

"One of you, however, will prove to the world that you are nothing but an actor, and you will be fired."

Cue the henhouse despair.

"And here is your challenge: Tonight you will attend a masquerade ball right here in the Plaza Hotel grand ballroom. It will be the party of the year, and you have the honor of being the only invited guests. Unfortunately, your perfect night will be crashed by ten imposters who will be disguised in costumes and masks just like you. Your job, my friends, is to separate the beautiful people from the impudent wannabes. You are allowed to ask any person you meet no more than three questions. When you are asked a question yourself, you can tell the truth, tell a lie, or tell anything in between. At the end of the night, the person who has identified the most imposters will choose who gets fired."

"Oh shit," said Cass, a little too loudly. She had expected a simple loser-gets-fired kind of arrangement. Now her exit strategy had suddenly become that much more difficult.

"Yes, Cassandra, did you have something to add?" said Micah.

"No...no...sorry...yes! I have a question. Are we allowed to fire ourselves?"

"Why would you want to do that, Cassandra? Is ten million dollars too low for you?" asked Micah.

The birdbrains laughed.

Yes, as a matter of fact, $10 million is too low, thought Cass, as she paced her cramped trailer later that afternoon. Only $10 million to commit suicide on *StarBash*? No, thank you. *StarBash* might have had zero Hollywood cred, but it had more than enough power to ruin her career. And when you added Brandi Bonacore, who would gladly plant a dagger in Cass's back if given half a chance, things looked even worse. No, just like Freddie, her agent, had warned, this lousy job had no upside. Of course, he only knew half the story, the half that didn't include the struggle with Lenora Danmore, but he had been right.

Cass had two choices: get off the show now, no matter how bad it looked, and possibly take a hit to her career; or, take a risk, possibly catastrophic, and try to go out in style by sticking around until she won one of the challenges. Cass had good business sense. Her career proved it. The fact that she knew how to make painful decisions also proved it. And she made one of those decisions that afternoon in the trailer. She was gone. Even if the exit she had in mind looked less than dignified, she was gone.

Brandi Bonacore liked being back on a big-time production, even if it had to be reality TV. She'd been out of action for too long. Three years to be exact. And during that time, she'd done exactly two fake courtroom shows and one fake dating show. That had been it. And she'd had to use a different name to even get those jobs. They paid two hundred dollars each. She had tried self-submitting video auditions for a while after her agent bailed and had even gotten some good-looking callbacks, but then somebody would whisper into somebody else's ear and the deal would die.

Brandi liked *StarBash*. Considering that she had been a little one-woman Hollywood basher in her own right, it only made sense. The show reminded her of the story of the king with no clothes, only in this case the king was full of shit, and *StarBash* showed it to the world every week. The other actors tried to have it both ways; when the cameras rolled, they played along, and when the cameras stopped, they trashed the show. Brandi didn't care. She'd already crossed the line and didn't plan on going back. And when one of the other actors got burned on the show, she didn't feel the least bit sorry. The way she looked at it, if you're a plastic person with a plastic personality, maybe it's not such a good idea to go near the fire.

In some ways, though, the whole *StarBash* thing didn't add up. Yeah, everyone in Hollywood had gotten the memo: if you cared about your career you stayed away. But the screwy thing was that because of the show's popularity, if a down-and-out actor dared to cross the line and did well on the show, then that suddenly popular rogue actor zoomed straight to the top, and the jobs came flooding in. And then, assuming a brain bigger than a walnut, the actor confessed his sins, fell back in line, and stayed as far away from *StarBash* as possible. The rules had a nasty bite, as Brandi knew better than anyone, but if you threw in enough money and power, things had a funny way of suddenly turning a little fuzzy.

All this meant that Brandi had a shot at erasing the damage from the last three years of her life. *StarBash* had the power to make it all disappear. And she figured what the hell. Somebody had to win. It also meant that she had a shot at getting even with the person who had ruined those years. And since *StarBash* had such off-the-charts ratings—fifty million people a week—with a little luck, she could pay back Cass Moreaux ten times in a single day. Maybe this would be that day.

She'd heard the other actors talking strategy for the masquerade ball, and it mostly involved weeding out the imposters with technical stuff: What is blocking? What is a POV shot? What does the second AD do? To Brandi all this sounded too simple. She knew this show, and these imposters weren't going to be just some dummies grabbed off the street.

They'd be carefully picked and coached enough to make things interesting. So Brandi decided to take a different path. She'd ask innocent-sounding questions that didn't seem to have right or wrong answers—unless you knew how things really worked, like she did.

By the time the event had finally wound down, Cass had carried out a plan that had been effective—and painfully clumsy. She had no doubt about either of those two points. And she had no regrets. Now the time had come to take her lumps, and that's what she planned to do. She'd follow the plan, take the calculated hit, and go home. She was ready.

The cameras rolled, and Micah, dressed in a tuxedo and bow tie, stepped onto the ballroom stage to reveal the winner to the unmasked actors, who had grouped in front of the stage. "Let it never be said that *StarBash* doesn't know how to throw a big-time Hollywood party!" he exclaimed.

Cass, still wearing a red wig and costume, clapped and screamed with the other Kool-Aid drinkers. She figured what the hell, she might as well go out with a bang.

"And that's what you are," continued Micah, "big-time! When fifty-three million people know your name, there is just no other way to put it. In fact, according to the Official Advertisers Scale of Celebrity, fifty-three million means that you are more famous than Jack the Ripper! Congratulations! By the way, Ronald McDonald is at fifty-four million, in case you want to shoot for something bigger."

The actors looked confused but clapped anyway.

"Yes, my friends," continued Micah. "Today you are famous. But the real question is, how famous will you be tomorrow? I'm sorry to say that for one of you, the answer is not very. That's right, the time has come to send one of you home. You have been challenged to weed out the imposters who crashed your exclusive Hollywood party. Now let's see how some of you decided to tackle the problem."

A film clip of the masquerade ball began playing on a screen that hung over the stage. As it played, two handheld Steadicams roved among the actors to catch their reactions to the film. A third stationary tripod camera in the very back captured the wide-angle master shot that included all the action and all the players. Cass resisted the urge to hide from all three of them. She squeamishly watched the film.

"What's a gaffer?" asked the first masked partygoer to another masked partygoer. The clip then showed this same question being asked forty or fifty times by a wide assortment of partygoers. It ended with a serious-sounding masked man offering his opinion: "The gaffer is the person responsible for catching gaffes. This person sits next to the director and yells, 'Gaffe!' whenever they catch one. They also bring the director coffee and medication."

The clip ended, the actors chuckled, and Cass breathed. *So far so good,* she thought.

"Who was that masked man?" asked Micah.

One of the actors raised his hand.

"Roddy Markem! Way to throw down the oil slick! Roddy is wearing number twelve. How many of you incorrectly listed him as an imposter?"

Most the actors raised their hands.

"That's right, seven of you did," said Micah. "We'll call you the techno-sleuths because you asked technical questions about gaffers and grips and best boys. Unfortunately, this strategy didn't work very well. The techno-sleuths on average nabbed only four imposters."

The actors sighed for the cameras.

"But don't feel bad," continued Micah. "Someone else did even worse. In fact, this special person didn't catch a single imposter."

All heads instantly snapped toward Cass. A crack army couldn't have been in more unison. The two Steadicams, one on each side, zoomed in on her face. *Here goes nothing,* she thought.

"My goodness, Cassandra, why are all your friends staring at you?" asked Micah.

"Just show the clip, Micah," said Cass.

He laughed and said, "Very good, Cassandra; you read my mind. Let's show the world your very original strategy."

The clip showed Cass with a red wig, freckles, mask, and prairie dress. She was supposed to be Anne of Green Gables. She wandered around the ballroom and asked every person she met her one big question, "If I pay you one hundred thousand dollars, will you fire me from this [bleep] show?" After showing three or four of these encounters, a carefully edited version of the same clip cut away the wandering and just showed her asking the question in a pathetic-sounding rapid succession. Then, since that had been so much fun, another edited version cut out everything else except the bleeped-out cuss word, which Cass repeated over and over and over again. And then it ended, and everyone laughed their asses off.

This is going worse than I had planned, thought Cass. She looked at Micah and knew at once that he had both barrels loaded. She braced herself.

"Anne of Green Gables! Such language!" he exclaimed. "It's a good thing Marilla isn't here, or you'd be eating soap for a week!"

More laughter. And he wasn't done.

"Now, Anne, a hundred thousand dollars is a lot of money. I hope you didn't steal Marilla's brooch to pay for it! You do remember what happened last time, don't you?"

One of the cameras panned the laughing mob while the other crowded up to Cass's face. If she tensed up she'd look like a stick of dynamite with a red wig, so she smiled and tried to roll with the punches. How convincing this was she didn't know. The ruckus eventually died down, and Micah continued.

"I have to tell you, Cassandra, we've had actors try to get off the show before but never quite like that. That was…interesting. How many takers did you get?"

"Everyone. All nine actors," said Cass.

"Well, I'm no mathematician," said Micah, "but that sounds to me like you might be going home."

Cass smiled for the cameras and said, "Yes, Micah. I believe that's what it means."

"Well, OK then," continued Micah. "I guess we better find out who gets the check and the big kiss goodbye." He turned his attention back to the whole group and continued, "OK, my friends. You heard it straight from our resident A-lister. She wants out and will pay one hundred thousand dollars to whoever gives her the boot. That means tonight one of you will collect a cool two hundred grand, including a hundred thousand dollars from *StarBash* for the charity of your choice and a hundred thousand dollars from Cassandra Moreaux that goes straight into your pocket. Are you ready to find out which one of you is the big winner?"

The actors clapped and hollered and pounded on the stage.

"Roddy Markem!" exclaimed Micah.

Roddy yelled, threw his fists into the air, and pushed his way toward the stage.

Then Micah continued: "You are not the winner, Roddy, but you did get second place. Congratulations."

Roddy's puffed-up chest sprang a leak, and he disappeared back into the crowd.

"The winner of this week's contest," continued Micah, "and the winner of the biggest cash prize ever awarded for a single challenge is..."

A handful of actors still in the running crowded up to the stage. They stood rigidly straight, with clinched fists and red faces.

"...Brandi Bonacore!"

Brandi pumped her fists repeatedly and launched into some sort of gyrating honky-tonk dance. The other actors also celebrated. It really represented the perfect outcome. Not everybody won, but everybody got another week on *StarBash*—except for Cass, the only person who didn't want it. So she joined the celebration, too. If she had had any doubt about the plan, it now vanished because nobody on earth wanted to see her get fired more than Brandi Bonacore. Even with the prime-time flogging Cass had just taken, she could honestly say that it couldn't have worked out any better.

Micah invited Brandi up to the stage. They had her in a Spanish Dulcinea costume that didn't work; she looked like two hundred pounds of Italian sausage squeezed into a hundred-pound casing. She had a round, streetwise face with jowls. Her black curly hair looked OK. Up until a few years ago, she'd made a good living playing the thirtysomething big-mouthed mistress in a few different mob movies or the sassy sidekick in several romantic comedies. Then she opened her mouth once too often and hit the skids.

"Now, Brandi," said Micah, "you threw down a pretty strange strategy tonight. You asked about politics, favorite movies, and, most strange of all, where people shop for groceries. What was that all about?"

"Let's just say it wasn't all that hard to weed out the imposters," said Brandi.

"And...?" coaxed Micah.

"And that's all I got to say."

"Uh...OK...well, you do have to say a bit more than that," said Micah. "You have to tell us about your charity, and then you have to fire someone. Can you do that?"

"Yep."

"Great. Why don't you start by telling us about your charity?"

"My charity is the National Rifle Association."

The actors gasped.

Brandi continued: "The National Rifle Association's mission is to protect and defend the Constitution of the United States, especially with reference to the inalienable right of the individual American citizen to acquire, possess, collect, exhibit, transport, carry, and enjoy the right to use arms."

"Uh...OK...let's give our audience some more details about your charity. Roll the video," said Micah.

The promo video played, but the actors didn't watch. They stared at Brandi. She returned their stare with an added measure of defiance. *And this woman wonders why she can't find work*, thought Cass. The end of the video was met with complete silence. Then Micah spoke solemnly.

"Brandi, do you have a college degree?"

"No."

"I'm sorry to hear that because I have to be honest with you. If you don't win *StarBash*, I don't think you're ever going to work in Hollywood again, and I wanted to hear that you had something to fall back on."

"That's OK, Micah. I haven't sold out yet, and I'm not gonna start now. I'm OK with it," said Brandi.

"You're a special person, Brandi, and I'm proud to know you," said Micah.

And then Brandi gave him a hug. *Two low IQs became one and maybe added up to a moron*, thought Cass.

"All right, it's time to fire somebody," continued Micah. "Sometimes our contestants find this part of the show to be difficult. But something tells me tonight might be a little different. Are you ready, Brandi?"

"You betcha."

And, just as Cass had expected, Brandi pointed at her and said, "Do you have my check, Cass?"

Did she ever. Cass held up the check and pushed to the apron of the stage. The monkey show had ended, and it made her want to scream with happiness. She handed the check to Brandi.

Brandi held up the check and smiled for the cameras. And then the smile faded into a frowning scowl. She looked down at Cass, who still stood just a few feet away. She said, "Cass Moreaux, this is what I think of your money." She dramatically tore the check into little pieces. The actors gasped loudly. Brandi continued: "And this is what I think of you." She bent down and blew the little pieces of paper into Cass's face and wig. The camera caught everything, including Cass's stunned expression. Brandi continued: "You ruined my life, Cass, and now the whole world is going to watch you pay for it, week after week. You're not going anywhere." Brandi stood up, pointed at Roddy, and said, "Sorry, Roddy, nothing personal, but you're a little too clever. You're fired."

What does a person do at this point? There just isn't an easy way to rehearse for the time when you will be insulted in front of fifty million people. So Cass stood there and took it. She didn't respond physically or verbally in any way. Of course she wanted to make Brandi pay for taking such a cheap shot, but Cass instinctively knew that she'd end up stooping just as low as Brandi. She had no choice but to submit to the camera's chokehold and to let Brandi glower at her. She also had to listen to Micah launch into a final round of jokes, all of them at her expense. Eventually the filming ended, but nobody moved. The cast and crew stood and stared at her, as if such a special occasion required her to say or do some particular thing. They must have been disappointed when Cass made only one quiet, simple statement to Brandi and then left.

After the ambush, as it quickly got dubbed when it exploded all over social media, Micah went back and watched the film. He didn't like what he saw. Brandi dropped the bomb on Cass, who obviously had been blindsided, and he proceeded to yuk it up from every possible angle. And then he closed the show with his usual ringmaster-from-hell routine. And fifty million people called it another fun night of television entertainment. What else could he have done?

Nothing. That's what *StarBash* did. That's what he did. Yes, he truly had no fondness for actors. And yes, he believed that *StarBash* sometimes asked legitimate questions. But did a reality-TV circus act really have any business trying to answer those questions? And, more importantly to Micah, had his shtick gotten so out of control that he'd morphed into some kind of cruel sideshow spectacle, a monster of his own creation?

And what about Cass, the one who'd taken a direct hit? Movie stars from the top of the heap are supposed to be rotten to the core. But she didn't respond like that. She displayed admirable composure and then, after the filming had ended, after she had voluntarily forfeited any hope of a televised counterattack, she calmly said, "I'm sorry you feel that way, Brandi. I hope we can find a way to work this out."

Somehow things had turned upside down. Micah had ended up looking like the obnoxious actor, and Cass looked like the levelheaded human being.

Micah had known from the beginning that he and *StarBash* didn't go well together. This kind of show needed an oily prankster who didn't really care one way or the other. That wasn't Micah. He cared. And, once the cameras started rolling, that sometimes caused him to add a little too much zing to the zingers.

In the beginning the show had been nothing but a quick way to raise money for Lenora's museum. So Micah agreed—contingent upon certain provisions regarding ownership. He had figured a run of two seasons, tops, and he'd be done. Now, four years later, Lenora and the network hounded him daily about seasons five and six. This dustup between Cass and Brandi, and yet another ratings surge, didn't make things any easier. Micah never knew success could look so bleak.

Immediately after the episode aired, the paparazzi invaded. Micah expected that. He didn't expect the rest of the press corps, who came out in even greater numbers. At first the story ran as a gossipy piece about a nasty feud that had erupted between two actors on national TV. Then it turned political, like most topics of conversation in the age of information. One side condemned the show for legitimizing a hate-monger and for allowing an actor of Cass's stature to be ambushed in such a cruel and unfair manner. The other side fired back that if Hollywood hadn't been such a cloistered swamp that suppressed the opinions of people like Brandi Bonacore, then this event never would have happened in the first place. Both sides accused each other of intolerance. At this point Micah didn't care anymore. He wanted it to be over.

Micah had been through rough patches before—Lenora never made things easy—but this patch felt a little rougher than most. But Micah plowed ahead, just as he'd always done. He also beefed up security and told them to keep the two ladies apart—except when the cameras rolled. That last part had been forcefully communicated to him by the money people.

Getting tossed from the crappy reality show was supposed to have been the easy part of Cass's plan. Instead, it had become a minefield that had knocked her on her ass after barely even a step. She knew the answer. She just didn't know how to make it happen. If she walked off the show, lawsuits would definitely follow, but she'd survive. Surviving the other fallout didn't look as good. Now that Brandi had thrown down the gauntlet, if Cass left she'd be tagged as a lightweight coward who had skedaddled as soon as things got tough. She'd be Cass the nasty bully versus Brandi the brave underdog. People liked these kinds of stories and didn't easily forget them. Her career might not ever recover. And if she stayed, she ran the risk of even more destruction. Cass felt completely lost.

And just as Cass knew the right answer—get the hell out of Dodge—so did all her friends and a few of her enemies, and they just had to share their epiphanies. So they called, one after the other, and told her what she already knew. Except for Freddie, her agent, he just cried on the phone.

The one call that offered the most hope also happened to be the one Cass least wanted to answer. It came from Lenora. The same Lenora who had an expertise in this type of damage control precisely because she'd had seventy years of experience evading the consequences of the crime she had committed against Cass's own mother! The irony made Cass want to scream. She took the call anyway. She felt that desperate.

CHAPTER SIX

Lenora sat on the bench and watched the afternoon waves break lazily onto the sand. In reality, she simply watched a film as it played on giant video monitors at the back of the set. They'd had to shoot new ocean footage at the same cove in Antibes where the original scene had been filmed, but it looked authentic. Even the color of the sky and the size of the waves perfectly matched the original movie. They had also brought in three truckloads of sand and had recreated the tall rock formation of the cove that framed the scene on the right and left. Of the fifteen interactive exhibits at the museum, Lenora liked this one best. The fact that the scene came from *Conspiracy to Commit Marriage*, winner of eleven academy awards, including best actress for Lenora, probably had something to do with her fondness.

On this day, however, Lenora liked the exhibit for an entirely different reason: it provided a soothing atmosphere for Cassandra Moreaux, the dumb little lamb who needed to continue down the chute, peacefully unaware that she had somewhere to go.

After a few minutes, Cassandra entered the set by way of the escalator. Lenora stood and watched expectantly to see how she responded to the exhibit, but Cassandra didn't look at it. She purposely ignored it. She chose a childish slight over artistic awareness. Given their current relationship, Lenora almost understood.

"Hello, Cassandra."

"Hello, Lenora."

The ladies stood silently. In acting, well-placed silence can provide emphasis, the difference between a dagger to the heart and a dagger to the heart with a twist. Lenora had a reputation as an acknowledged expert of the pause, and she didn't use it just in the movies. She smiled patiently and waited for Cassandra to feel the silence, which she did.

"You had something to tell me about Brandi?" she finally asked.

"Yes, I do. Shall we sit here and enjoy an afternoon at the beach?"

They sat on the bench.

"I've spoken to Brandi, and she is willing to end her war with you," said Lenora, who then waited for a response. It didn't come. If anything, Cassandra looked unhappy. Lenora asked, "Is there something you don't like about this news?"

"Everyone knows I want off the show. I was hoping you had something for me along those lines," said Cassandra.

"Actually, I do, dear. It's some simple advice that says a graceful exit is better than a quick, ugly exit, and that's what I'm offering. This deal will turn down the heat while you search for a graceful exit."

"OK. What does Brandi want from me?" said Cassandra.

"I'll get to that," said Lenora, "but first let me explain that if we make this deal, the feud will continue to be front and center on the show—the ratings are too good to let it go—but she won't say anything specific about your past dealings together. It will be more of an ongoing general animosity."

"So instead of being a big bitch, she'll just be a little bitch; is that what you're saying?"

"Reality-TV runs on bitches and idiots, dear, as I'm sure you already know," said Lenora.

"No. But I'm learning fast. Now what does she want?"

"She doesn't want anything...at least not from you. She wants a co-executive producer credit for next season, and I'm willing to give it to her because there's something you can do for me," said Lenora.

"And what is that?"

"I want you to accept an invitation to the museum's grand opening. It will be held on Friday, June 5, and it's important that the right people are here. All the major media will be present, and I need big names and pretty faces for them to admire. And since the grand opening is the day after *StarBash* wraps for the season, you can just stay another night and save yourself the extra travel."

"It's a nice thought, but *StarBash* and I will be parting company long before that," said Cassandra.

"Oh, I don't know. You might surprise yourself. Something tells me that underneath all that Actors Studio intensity lies the heart of a true reality star," said Lenora, with an innocent smile.

"Thank you," said Cassandra, who obviously recognized the little jab. Then she said, "Is that all you want, Lenora, just the museum grand opening?"

"That's all."

"Because if I agree, it won't change anything about what we talked about before or what I'll do when I get the proof I'm looking for. Which reminds me, when am I getting a copy of your birth certificate?"

"It's already been ordered from Milwaukee County. They said it takes six weeks," said Lenora.

"That's funny. When we talked before, you said it had to be ordered from a foreign country," said Cassandra.

"Did I say that? I don't know where my brain is these days. Anyway, not to worry, it's all taken care of. Now listen, Cassandra. I know you are serious about what happened to your mother, and, don't think I'm being flippant, but the results of your search don't really concern me. I don't have anything to hide, and eventually you will find that out. In the meantime, I have a museum to open, you have a career to protect, and it just so happens that if we work together, we can accomplish both of those things. It's just good business, especially with a loose cannon like Brandi Bonacore in the mix. Do we have a deal?"

Brandi's pie hole had been plugged, and so, in that regard, the world looked a little brighter when Cass left the museum that afternoon. Lenora, on the other hand, baffled Cass. She had blatantly changed her story—regarding the foreign country—but continued to assert her innocence and act as carefree as a porpoise in a fish farm. Cass didn't buy it. In fact, the possibility of a birth certificate from a foreign country had already climbed to the top of Cass's suspicious list, and she had taken appropriate action. Lenora had two legal names at her disposal: her stage name, Lenora Danmore, and her supposed birth name, Carolyn Anna Voyt. But neither of those two names had shown up in the FBI files. A birth certificate with a third name that no one knew about might be the answer to the puzzle. And now that Lenora had started backtracking, Cass had become more suspicious than ever.

As she started down the footpath that led to the trailers, Cass noticed a flickering light in Micah's workshop. It reminded her that she had another piece of unfinished business with a certain smart-ass who'd had just a little too much fun at her expense. There's having fun, and then there's piling on, and apparently the Tinseltown tyrant didn't know the difference. She decided a friendly social call might be in order.

Cass approached the door and heard laughing and talking inside. She knocked. The laughing and talking continued, but no one answered the door. She stepped to her left and peeked in the window. She saw a dark workshop except for the flickering light from a computer monitor on Micah's desk. It played some sort of video, and that was also where the voices seemed to be coming from. Cass's devilish imagination instantly kicked into gear, and she wondered about the video. Was it a classic car video or some other video having to do with the museum? Or, heaven forbid, could it be a movie-movie, featuring a real-life cast of reprobate actors with plastic faces and bad boob jobs? Had the terminator backslidden and fallen prey to Hollywood's evil snare? She stepped back to the entrance and tried the doorknob. It turned. She looked over her shoulder to make sure no one witnessed her little spy mission and then slipped inside.

She quickly determined the place to be empty and headed straight to the monitor on Micah's desk. Unfortunately, the video in question turned out to be nothing but a home movie. But then she looked closer and realized that not just any family starred in this home movie. It featured Lenora and a man and a little boy. Lenora and the man looked to be in their late thirties or early forties, and the boy looked about two or three years old. Now Cass's curiosity had really been piqued. Lenora had been married and divorced at a very young age. After that she never remarried and had never had any children. The man didn't look like anyone that had been publicly connected to Lenora or anyone that had been in the industry at that time that Cass knew about. Something just didn't make sense. Cass watched some more. Lenora balanced a wicker basket on her head and did an Irish jig at the same time. For some reason she felt the need to put on a show for the boy. The man knelt down and gently pushed the reluctant boy toward Lenora. He said, "Look at Mother. Maybe she has your present in the basket." The boy clung to the man's arm. The man kept pushing and said, "Come on, Micah, go see what mother has in the basket."

Cass stood up ramrod straight. *Micah? Mother?* She paused the video and looked over at the pictures on the wall that she'd seen the other day. Those pictures showed Micah as a little boy. He'd admitted it. She grabbed one of the pictures, returned to the monitor, and compared the two images. It was Micah. He looked younger in the video but it was definitely Micah.

And now the whole twisted story made sense. Why had a superstar like Lenora hired a manager who had barely graduated high school? Why had she fired him a thousand times but had always taken him back? Why had Micah stuck with Lenora these last ten years after her career had ended? Because Micah the manager didn't even exist! Micah the obsessively devoted employee had been a smoke screen! It answered all the questions, including the granddaddy of them all: Why did Micah Bailey hate actors? Because Micah Bailey had his very own *Mommy Dearest,* and her name was Lenora Danmore! If you searched the slimiest tabloids for a year, you'd never come up with a better answer than that.

Cass sat down in Micah's chair and let her brain play tug-of-war with the revelation. Aside from the obvious fact that Lenora had had a baby very late in life, Cass also understood the how and why of it from a professional point of view. Back then major actors lived very controlled and scripted public lives. How they dressed, who they dated, and where they went had more to do with marketing than personal preference. And you never, ever let the public see your dirty laundry, and that included your illegitimate love child. That part of it all made sense. But what about everyday life? How had Lenora been able to live that out? A child, not to mention the child's father, might be successfully stashed away for a few hours when the cameras are rolling, but what do you do with them during the weeks, months, and years that come in between? What had Lenora done with Micah all the years before the actor-and-manager charade had begun? Knowing Lenora, the answer to that question wouldn't be the subject of a heartwarming movie anytime soon.

As Cass's mind pondered these questions, her eyes got distracted by a framed photograph sitting on Micah's desk. It showed a beautiful young woman with blonde hair, tan face, and a light smattering of freckles. She looked like a California surfer girl. Cass wondered who she might be. Sister, girlfriend...but not wife because Micah's marriage had ended some years ago...or so Cass had heard.

She refocused her thoughts and looked back at the mother and child. Now, for some reason, the video felt different. The mother offered clownish enticement, and the boy resisted, the same way any three-year-old resists being pushed to a stranger. Lenora had no natural connection to her child, so she resorted to the only connection she understood: actor and audience. The video made Cass feel sad, as did the fact that Micah even had it on his computer. If any human being needed something better to watch, it had to be Micah Bailey. And then Cass got an idea. She grabbed the computer mouse, opened her favorite online movie site, and cued up *Planes, Trains & Automobiles*. He had the car from that movie in the collection, so she figured she'd give it a try. She scribbled out a note and taped it to the monitor. It said, *Don't worry; you're not watching a movie! You're doing research on one of your cars. Enjoy! Cass.*

Micah heard approaching footsteps. The door opened, sunlight poured over him like a spotlight, and Cass saw him sitting in the swivel chair just inside her trailer. She gasped and said, "Shit! Micah! You scared me!" She stepped up into the trailer. "What the hell are you doing in here? It's not right."

"Do you mean kind of like this?" said Micah, as he held up his phone for Cass to see. It showed a video of Cass sneaking into Micah's workshop earlier that afternoon.

"You didn't lock your door," said Cass.

"Neither did you," said Micah.

"OK. You got me...but it still feels creepy...and why do you have that shit on your phone anyway?" She sat at the u-shaped dinette, just a few feet away.

Micah swiveled the swivel chair so that it faced Cass and said, "Because I get paid to stay one step ahead, and if I don't, Lenora will run me over and never look back. And she'll do the same thing to you. And that's one of the reasons I'm here. You had another meeting with her, and you didn't tell me about it. Listen, I can't make you do anything, but I can give you a warning. Lenora likes to make deals with people who think they can outsmart her. Don't do it."

"Uh...OK...you do know she's a hundred years old, right?"

"Eighty-seven and more dangerous than ever. I just thought you should know," said Micah.

"OK, so now I know. What else do you want?" said Cass.

"To know if you'll have dinner with me?"

When Cass flinched like she'd been hit with a spit wad, Micah knew the organic appeal of his invitation had certain deficiencies, an impression that Cass quickly confirmed.

"Uh...no! Why would you even ask that?"

"Because you're not what you're supposed to be...you're not what I expected...and I find that very interesting," said Micah.

"Uh...OK, that was creep-out number two, but I'm going to let it pass because you are obviously a little challenged in that department."

"Thank you."

"Micah, you and I are as different as two people could ever be. I mean, really, it's scary to even think how different we are."

"So, you don't have dinner with people who are different? That sounds very...homogenized...and boring."

"Thank you for your concern, but I'm sure I'll survive. Now if that's all..."

"Not quite. I also owe you an apology, and since I won't be doing it over the best barbecue in California, I'll do it now. I stepped over the line the other night with that whole Brandi thing, and I'm sorry. I should've tried to give you a fair footing, but I hammed it up instead. That's what this show does to me sometimes and...anyway..." He stood up and stepped over to the door.

"Thank you, Micah, that means a lot to me." She stood up. "It upset me, too, but now that you've explained, it makes sense. It's the pressure of the cameras and the need to perform. The same thing has happened to me. Thank you." She extended her hand. He started to reach for it, but she withdrew it.

He withdrew his hand. She gave him a quick, awkward hug. And then he started to leave. Before Cass closed the door, he turned and said, "What did you want anyway? When you went to the workshop?"

"You know, I can't remember. I guess it couldn't have been that important."

Before the question had even popped out of his mouth, Cass knew the answer had to be no. Her career had already taken a beating. The last thing it needed was rumors of a romance with Micah Bailey. Despite his part in the legend of Lenora Danmore and despite their many successes, Micah Bailey had now become the face of *StarBash*, and Hollywood hated *StarBash*. She didn't need to be attached to that kind of stigma. It didn't make business sense. So she'd made up a quick excuse. It had been mostly true but maybe a little incomplete.

Later that night, after the unnerving trauma of his invitation had worn off, Cass thought about the assessment she had made of Micah before she had barely met him. It had been convenient for her to peg him as a simpleton and put him in the enemy camp, but now she knew that it hadn't been entirely accurate. He clearly possessed a sharp, well-spoken wit. And he put it on display week after week. You didn't have to be a fan to admit that much. Even the enemy tag didn't seem to be a perfect fit. He bashed Hollywood, no doubt about that, but he did it with Hollywood actors, a Hollywood crew, and on a show that ran once a week for seventeen straight weeks on Hollywood network TV. The guy had a lot of Hollywood in and around him. Maybe *enemy* hadn't been the right word. Maybe he was just a different cog in the big Hollywood wheel. Or maybe she was just looking for excuses because when he dropped the TV shtick, she found him to be genuinely likable. Sure, he sometimes took a narrow view of things, but Cass also found him to be funny, sincere, and not too narrow-minded to admit when he'd made a mistake.

Overall there was an attraction—Cass felt it—but it had more to do with her sad state of affairs than anything about Micah personally. He just happened to fit into a particular mold, a kind of prototype. In fact, if someone rounded up a dozen more just like him, decent men who didn't know her, who hadn't seen any of her movies, and who didn't particularly like her, Cass would gladly pay top dollar for the lot and then sort through them until she found the man of her dreams. As crude as this sounded, it also showed how difficult the dating scene could be for someone in the public spotlight. Every man she met thought they knew her. After all, they'd seen every one of her movies—ten times each. In this type of relationship, Cass the movie star reigned queen, and

Cass the person amounted to an unwanted guest. The good times lasted until Cass the person poked her head in once too often.

If you fall in love and marry a man who you've known since college, you can sidestep this kind of problem, but that doesn't mean there won't be other problems, like an affair with a network meteorologist. Cass had learned about her husband's infidelity from Freddie, her agent, who had learned about it when one of the tabloids called just before running a front-page picture of her husband frolicking at the beach with the bombshell weathergirl. When Cass found out the affair had been going on for the entire five-year marriage, she filed for divorce. She had now been divorced for three years. During that time her career had continued to flourish, and she had achieved the success that she had always dreamed about. In her personal life, though, she felt like anything but a success.

So there you had it, the current state of Cassandra Moreaux's love life, the long and short of it being that her ex-husband knew the weather report better than a sea captain, the last three years had been shitty, and Micah Bailey took home the prize for being the best romantic prototype of the batch...and an undeniable career killer.

CHAPTER SEVEN

"And here's your *StarBash* host, the Tinseltown terminator himself, Micah Bailey!"

"Hello, America, and welcome to *StarBash 2020*! Last week we threw the party of the year, and our movie stars dazzled all night long, even letting loose with some unexpected fireworks at the end. To reward them for a job well done, we let the actors choose this week's activity, and they unanimously voted to take a vacation. So we stocked the limo, loaded up our little troupe of plastic pretenders, and we hit the road. And then disaster struck. The limo broke down. And it didn't break down in a convenient place like Manhattan or Scarsdale or Old

Greenwich. It broke down right here, on good ol' Main Street USA.

"I'm standing in front of Joe's Jingletown Tavern. Jingletown is a factory bar in a factory town that has lost all of its factories. At one time, the factories on this street alone provided jobs to over ten thousand workers. If you drive it today, you will find five miles of boarded-up buildings and a street that employs less than three hundred workers. That's the bad news. The good news is that Joe's Jingletown is still here, and our beloved actors have a place to rest while their limo gets repaired. Let's go inside and see how they're coping with this tragic ordeal."

Bakersfield in the middle of the night, that's how far Cass had fallen, and it didn't seem possible that her foul mood could turn any more rancid. Then she saw the inside of the bar. If Joe's Jingletown Tavern sounded even remotely like a pleasant destination, then it needed to be renamed. Immediately. A better name might've been Joe's Black Mold Lounge or Joe's Too Broke Too Buy Sanitizer. And the handful of customers who slouched at the bar didn't do much to enhance the atmosphere. They wore dirty work clothes and, judging by the aroma, an alarming degree of hygienic neglect.

Cass stood with the others in front of a small stage, waiting to shoot Micah's challenge to them. Brandi stood off a few feet from the group, brewing in her perpetual persecution complex. At one point she'd said, "So how much are you offering this week, Cass? Hopefully the price has gone up after your big flop last week."

If she'd hoped to get a laugh out of the group, it didn't work. Cass ignored her, as did everyone else.

A microphone on a stand had been placed at the front of the scruffy-looking stage, and an old upright piano sat at the back, against the wall. The piano had been thoroughly pasted with old bumper stickers. One said, "I Shot J. R." Another said, "Billy Beer & Pork Rinds, Breakfast of Fat Champions." A sorry-looking guitar rested against the side of the piano. Opposite the stage, behind where the actors stood, the bartender had stacked chairs onto half a dozen small tables and was currently mopping the floor with dirty water. Overgrown red sideburns framed his skinny face, and he grumbled with each stroke of the mop. No one in the bar had acknowledged the actors' entrance earlier that evening. *Tuxedos and evening gowns—their attire for the night—must be a common occurrence in this fine establishment*, thought Cass. Or they'd been hired by *StarBash* and told exactly how to play it out. Or they really didn't give a shit—which also described Cass's attitude. She just wanted the cameras to roll and to get it over with, which finally started happening at a little past midnight. It was Micah time, every redneck's favorite time of day.

He boldly pushed through the swinging doors like he'd just made history at the O. K. Corral. After a brief, somber pose for the cameras, he moseyed to the microphone on the stage and addressed the actors.

"Wow! Look how things have changed! Last week, my dear stranded thespians, your playground was a luxurious grand ballroom with an orchestra and flowing champagne. This week it's a dive bar, a jukebox, and cheap beer. Isn't it strange how life throws these curveballs at us?

"But maybe it's not strange at all. Maybe it's divine intervention. After all, the only way to win *StarBash* is to successfully travel from the very top of society all the way down to the very bottom. Maybe Joe's Jingletown Tavern is meant to be part of that journey? Maybe this is where you will prove to America that you are more than just actors. What do you say, team? Do you want to give it a try?"

The group clapped compliantly.

"Actors, please say hello to Walter." Micah pointed to the bartender with the mop and then said, "Walter has agreed to judge our competition. Isn't that right, Walter?"

"Like I told the lady with the clipboard and the spike in her nose, I got a bar to close. I'll judge your contest, but I got a bar to close, and that comes first."

"Absolutely, Walter, you close your bar, and whatever you have left for our fearless players will be fine." Micah turned to a different camera. "And, just in case there's a tie or Walter gets too busy scraping gum off the floor, over here at the bar we have six of Jingletown's best customers, and they have graciously volunteered to be our alternate judges. Gentlemen, please say hello to our audience by waving to the cameras."

The men at the bar stayed hunched over their drinks with their backs to the world. They displayed an impressive assortment of plumber's cracks but didn't wave to anybody.

"As you can see," continued Micah, "our alternate judges are men of extreme focus." He turned back to the group. "Actors! Do you know that all of you have something special in common? That's right, all of you have won at least one competition that required you to make a speech. Between the nine of you, we have winners of beauty pageants, Daytime Emmys, Emmys, and even an Oscar. And tonight it is my privilege to announce that *StarBash*, in cooperation with Joe's Jingletown Tavern, will be transporting each of you back to that very moment when the historic envelope got torn open and the presenter proclaimed your name to the world. You are going to experience the ecstasy all over again, including the tearful gasp, the walk of fame, and the immortal speech that you shared with the world. And let me tell you this right now. Some of you are going shine extra bright tonight. I can just feel it. Your movie-star magnetism is going to zap that mop right out of Walter's hands and magically whisk him out of Joe's Jingletown Tavern and straight to the glittery world of a genuine Hollywood production! Are you ready to do that?"

The actors clapped eagerly and hugged one another with excitement. Cass felt her brain cells dying a billion at a time.

"Now, actors," continued Micah, "we have your original speeches all printed up, and your challenge is to recreate the magic as it actually happened. Walter will judge the content of your speech as well as the quality of delivery. Are you ready, Walter?"

"Yeah, I guess so," said Walter, without bothering to look up from his mopping.

And Cass was ready, too, because she completely understood the game at hand. *StarBash* planned to make them look like complete idiots. *Come one, come all, come see the self-absorbed rich actress stand in a stinking shithole while dressed in a sequined evening gown and diamond tiara. Watch her gush about all the "little people" to a bored man with a mop. Watch the world-famous butt-crack brothers turn their backs on her.* The only thing missing from this freak show was a flashing sign that said, *Genuine Hollywood Narcissist Now on Display*. Cass saw it all very clearly and intended to have nothing to do with it. She'd read her speech—since she saw no reasonable way out of it—but she'd read it like a brain-dead zombie. With any luck she would stink it up enough to get fired.

The actors took their seats around the rickety round tables where Walter had just mopped. He kept mopping in another section of the room. The lights dimmed, a spotlight illuminated the microphone, and the *StarBash* announcer's voice reverberated through the little bar. He said, "Ladies and gentlemen, presenting the award for outstanding supporting actor in a daytime drama series, please welcome Micah Bailey!"

A few of the actors clapped, but Micah bounced into the spotlight like it had been a standing ovation. He wore a big smile, and Cass knew he had to be enjoying this shit. He dramatically tore open a big black envelope and said, "And the winner is...Calvin Robbs!" Calvin, who sat at the table next to Cass, jumped to his feet. But then Micah said, "Unfortunately, Calvin is currently in rehab and is unable to join us this evening. Here to accept the award on behalf of Calvin Robbs is his mother, Golde Silverman."

The actors offered a smattering of confused applause, Calvin sat down, and an old lady with a gray bun on the top of her head stepped into the spotlight. She wore a sagging green sweater with bulging pockets over a nondescript knee-length print dress. Her nylon stockings had gathered just above the tops of her tan therapy shoes. The microphone towered two feet over her head. She stared at it like it had just insulted her. Micah lowered it. She spoke into the microphone and said, "So who is this Calvin Robbs, anyway? Such a big shot, making up fancy names and taking home shiny trophies. All his life he was Clarence Rothstein, a good boy who wanted to be a dentist, and then he went to live with his father in California, and this is what you get. But who am I? Just his mother, so I'll do what he said. I wrote it down so I'll do it. Just a second." She rummaged through one of her sweater pockets, and then the other. Calvin groaned. She finally retrieved a folded piece of paper. She unfolded the paper and tried unsuccessfully to read it. She put on the reading glasses that hung on a chain around her neck and, after clearing her throat, read the speech, which said, "Thank you for this award and goodbye." Then she left the stage. Calvin slumped in his seat like a man who'd just been convicted of murder.

The regular lights came back up. Micah retook the stage, and his smile had grown. Cass knew that smile. She had personally experienced it. Micah smelled blood in the water. He said, "Wow, Calvin, so many things going on here. Let's start with the way you jumped up when I called your name. Did you forget that your mom had to accept the award for you?"

Calvin rubbed his eyes and didn't answer.

"Very good," said Micah. "We'll take that as a definitive 'I don't want to talk about it.' Let's move on to the speech...er...if you can call it that. It had a beginning and an ending but not much in the middle. But maybe that's just me. Let's see what our judge has to say. Walter?"

Walter leaned against his mop like Moses leaning against his staff and said, "I liked it. From now on I think it should only be the moms and dads. It makes things more interesting. In ten seconds I figured out why he ran off to California, why he changed his name, and why he has to go to rehab. And I liked the speech, too. It was the perfect length. On the Budweiser six-pack scoring scale, I give it four out of six Budweisers."

"OK...wow...very good...that's a bit of a surprise," said Micah. "Let's check in with our alternate judges to get their feedback."

The camera panned over to the men at the bar just in time to catch absolutely nothing.

"Very good, gentlemen, keep up the good work," said Micah. Then he turned to Calvin, who's green complexion had improved somewhat. "Wow! Calvin

Robbs! You just scored four Budweisers. What do you have say about that?"

Calvin raised a timid fist into the air, and that was pretty much how the rest of the night unfolded. One by one *StarBash* portrayed the actors as self-indulgent idiots who didn't even have enough sense to know they were idiots. Except for Brandi. Her blue-collar crassness sold well in Joe's Jingletown Tavern. She got five Budweisers and blessed the world with another one of her honkytonk dances.

Cass's speech came from her best actress academy award, and she'd correctly guessed that *StarBash* would save it for last. She'd also assumed that since each of her colleagues had survived their ambush in the spotlight, more or less, she would, too. That had been a mistake, which she soon found out.

"Presenting the award for best actress in a leading role, please welcome Micah Bailey."

Micah opened the envelope, called her name, and Cass walked to the stage—no smile, no emotion, and hopefully no satisfaction for *StarBash*. *Let them eat zombie shit.* Just to cause maximum aggravation, she held the printed speech high enough to keep the cameras from getting a clear shot of her face. And then she read it like a dyslexic first grader. She made it as painful as humanly possible.

"Thank you. Thank you. Thank you. I am so overwhelmed right now. I forgot everything I wanted to say. One thing I will never forget, though, is the day Harold Wasser handed me the script for *Megabit* and introduced me to a little hurricane named Sassie Manners. She changed my life that day, and she has not stopped yet. Thank you, Harold. Oh...so many others...thank you to Danny Myers and the rest of the gang at BFD Productions. Thank you to Joel Rooney and Rachel York and Rick Sprague and Karen Powell and Val Dedic and Ralph Maloof and Kim Laurela and Barn Hendricks and...Freddie Garcielo and...and...if I left you out, please forgive me. You know I love you. I love all of you. I never worked so hard on anything in my life. We literally slogged through eighteen-hour days for six straight exhausting weeks. And I'd do it all over again in a heartbeat. That is how much I love this character. Thank you...thank you." She left the stage like a robot, just as she'd entered it, and sat back in her chair.

Micah said, "OK, thank you, Cassandra Moreaux, for reading the phone book to us. The whole world is now truly inspired. Hopefully, Walter will be able to choke back the tears long enough to give us your score. Walter?"

The cameras focused on Walter. He looked different. For some reason the grumbling drudgery had suddenly ceased. He now stood at attention and appeared agitated. His white knuckles shook as they choked the life out of the mop handle. Then they released their grip, and the mop fell to the floor with a loud bang. He looked at Cass with piercing eyes and said, "Listen, young lady, I got something to tell you. You got a lot of things most of us can't never even dream about, and maybe you deserve them, but that don't mean you can take what don't belong to you. You dance, and you sing, and you pretend. And we pay money to see you do it. And we work hard for that money. Harder than you'll ever know, and I don't care if you put in eighteen-hour days or twenty-four-hour days. It don't compare. I hated your speech because you tried to take what don't belong to you. One Budweiser, and I'm done with this shit." And then he walked away, exiting through a swinging door by the bar counter.

Both Steadicams immediately surrounded Cass. She held up her head and looked straight ahead but could feel the other actors staring at her. Micah stared at her. Her emotions had been raw all night, and she finally broke. She said, "Really? I said I worked hard, so he storms out. I'm sorry, but that doesn't exactly sound like the crime of the century!"

Nobody said a word. The cameras zoomed ever closer, hoping to capture any little nuance of guilt, begging for a full-blown meltdown. After a few seconds, in a quiet, hesitant voice, Micah said, "Cass, when a person gets paid millions of dollars for a two-month job, most people aren't going to be interested in hearing about how difficult the work was. But you're right, there is no crime here. You made an innocent statement that someone, for some reason, didn't want to hear. Nothing more than that." He then disconnected his body mic and said, "That's it for me, guys. Let's do the rest back at the ranch." He looked sad.

On the drive back, Cass tried to let it go. She told herself that she had done nothing but hit a sore spot on a man who was probably excessively prickly. The real blame belonged to *StarBash,* but, of course, they didn't care. Their exploitation bullshit had boiled over, and the cameras had scooped it up, just the way they had planned. And then Cass got an idea. She'd turn the tables on those shitheads and give them something really special to scoop up, and she'd give it to them Hollywood style. She unbuckled her seatbelt, stood up in the aisle, and yelled, "Stop the van!"

Micah got a call from the first AD, who had hitched a ride in one of the production trucks. She said, "Uh...Micah...I think we have a problem. Cass Moreaux jumped out of the actors' van and looks like she's heading back to the bar."

Micah, who'd been the director for that night's segment, said, "OK...get a camera on her and trail her...and make sure she stays safe. I'll get everyone turned around."

Micah and the lighting truck that carried him caught up with Cass about a half mile from the bar. She walked quickly and had a dozen strangers following along. At first this alarmed Micah—Cass had chosen to pull this stunt late at night and on the bad side of town—but then he watched her dart into a twenty-four-hour gasoline mini-mart and come out with six more people who seemed to happily follow along. Over the next several blocks, and after quick forays into another gas station, a taco stand, and a twenty-four-hour veterinary clinic, she steadily added to the group so that by the time she pushed into Joe's Jingletown, Cass had rounded up a party of thirty or forty people.

"Does anyone have a knife?" Those comforting words greeted Micah when he reentered the bar. Cass had said them, and she now stood onstage with the old guitar in her hands. The Steadicams had the scene covered, and the rest of the crew had everything under control, so Micah relaxed against the back wall with the rest of the actors.

One of Cass's posse, who had taken seats at the bar and around the tables, stood up and whipped out a large hunting knife.

"Mister, I said a knife, not a machete," said Cass.

"Ah...this ain't nothin'. You should see my other one," said the knife wielder.

The crowd laughed. Cass said, "No thanks. That will do. Come up here and cut open my dress."

The crowd hooted. The man came up onstage, and Cass showed him where to cut a slit in her evening gown. He smiled deviously for the crowd and obliged. Then she pushed him off the stage. Now Cass had some room to move. She put one foot up on the seat of a chair and straddled the guitar on her knee. She also exposed a portion of leg in the process. The crowd hooted some more. Shortly after this, the alternate judges at the bar abandoned their pledge of stoicism and turned around to watch the action. Walter, the prickly bartender, watched suspiciously as he scurried back and forth with foamy glasses of beer and shots of whiskey.

Cass calmly tuned the guitar and chatted with the audience.

She said, "What do you call a debutante with a broken nail? Depressed."

The crowd offered up some groans and a few laughs.

"What do you call a debutante with five broken nails and a black eye? A prostitute."

More groans and laughs.

"What do you call a debutante with ten broken nails? A car payment for Trang Nguyen."

That one got mostly laughs.

"Hey, did you hear about the cowboy who rode his horse into the saloon?

"The bartender said, 'Get that damn horse outta here.'

"The cowboy said, 'But he's a seeing-eye horse.'

"The bartender said, 'Who you bullshittin', mister? You ain't blind.'

"'Yeah, but I will be in about three hours.'"

More laughs. Cass gave the tune-up a final strum and said, "I'd like to play an old Johnny Cash song for you. It's called 'Don't Take Your Guns to Town.' The audience responded enthusiastically, including the six wise men at the bar. Even Walter flashed something that resembled a smile. Micah reached over to a small bank of light switches and dimmed the house lights. Cass gave him a quick wink, and Micah marveled at her composure. *Seriously, how long has it been since this lady played a Johnny Cash song in front of an audience*? he wondered. *And now she's up there like it's just the next stop on a six-month tour.*

Cass plucked a single note on the guitar. The audience quieted. The easy humor on Cass's face became sober and reflective. She plucked another note, and another, and then she sang the ballad about a gun, a cowboy, and a mother's love. The audience leaned into it, following every step of the way, until Cass finally strummed out the mother's sad plea one last time as her son lay dead on the floor. And then it ended, but the audience waited one beat, two beats, three beats before applauding. Nobody wanted to break the spell, so they waited until the dam burst under its own weight.

"How 'bout if we add a little pepper sauce to this party?" asked Cass.

The room responded with cheers and whistles and applause.

"The song is called 'Jackson,' and I need some help with it. What about you, Walter? Do you know that song?" Cass looked at Walter, and so did everyone else.

"That song's been in the jukebox for fifty years, and I ain't a moron, so what do you think?" said Walter.

"Good, then get your ass up here, and help me out!" said Cass.

Walter threw down his bar towel and hustled up to the stage.

And then they sang, and they sang like the moment had been made for them. Two people from worlds so far apart that it hardly seemed worthwhile even acknowledging each other's existence. But here they were now, side by side, ignoring reality, creating a new existence that fit perfectly into their current time and place. Micah saw this, and for the first time in his life he recognized a different kind of human connection that was intimate and fleeting, senseless and void of expectation. It drank the wine of here and now because tomorrow the intoxicating moment would be long gone. Two people had stepped onto a ledge together, bolstered by nothing more than a willingness to take a chance on an opportunity that promised to quickly disappear forever. To Micah it felt vulnerable, admirable, and unfamiliar.

And who had been the instigator of this unusual brand of brotherly love? Cass Moreaux. Granted, after the earlier problem, maybe she thought she had a point to prove, but she didn't have to throw herself out there like this. And then she actually pulled it off. She connected, not just with Walter but with Walter and everyone else she had packed into the place. Micah had caught a glimpse of this geniality before, when Cass had been goofing around with the guys in the shop, but now he saw it more clearly. She had once again turned his expectations upside down.

The duet had been a good finish to an eventful day, at least that's what Micah had assumed. The clock on the wall read 2:00 a.m., alcohol curfew, and the time had come to clear everyone out. But then again, Cass was a performer, and every performer has to have a big finish, so what happened next shouldn't have been much of a surprise. As the clapping and stomping and whistling died down, Walter leaned into the microphone, jabbed his finger at the camera, and said, "I want to change my vote. This lady here gets six Budweisers, and in my book, she deserves every one of them!"

"Thank you, Walter, that means a lot to me, and I'll cherish this moment for the rest of my life." She gave him a kiss on the cheek, fuzzy sideburns and all, and then said, "I also have something to say, to the people at *StarBash*. I want you to take a good look at what happened tonight because this is exactly what actors around the world do every day. We give people something to sing about. We give them something to look at besides problems. And when we're done, sometimes their problems don't look quite as big as they did before. And sometimes that's all it takes to make it through another day. We're not perfect, but we try our best, and we deserve some respect. There, now you heard it, but I'm sure it won't do any good because as far as I'm concerned, you are nothing but a bunch of ignorant assholes."

Cass won that week's contest. Micah announced it to the world but not until after the producers had huddled with her to explain that the official rules had been clarified so that winning actors were not permitted to fire themselves. And, furthermore, firing Brandi Bonacore had also been taken off the table because she had been granted a *StarBash* "death voucher"...on account of her win the previous week. It didn't take a great imagination to see through all this: Cass had her eye on the exit; the producers had to stop her at any cost, so they "clarified" the rule. And then they invented the handy-dandy "death voucher" to protect their other asset. Neither Cass nor Brandi would be going home anytime soon.

And the big insult that Cass had hurled at *StarBash*—the sincerity of which Micah admired—probably didn't have the effect Cass had hoped. Not only did it survive the cutting table and make it into the episode, but they even used snippets of it in the weekly television commercial to promote the episode. The audience loved it, and the ratings climbed even higher. Cass had poked the beast in the eye, and the beast had turned it to gold.

CHAPTER EIGHT

One evening, a few days after they had shot the bar episode, Cass found the door to her trailer unlocked even though she could have sworn that she had locked it. She muttered Micah's name under her breath and flung it open, expecting to find the tinhorn terminator sitting in the swivel chair. He wasn't there. She felt disappointed. Then she felt weird because she felt disappointed.

She did find an unfamiliar laptop opened up on the dining table. It had a note taped to the edge of the screen. Cass sat down at the table and read the note. Then she smiled. It seemed Mr. Bailey wanted to play a little game of dueling videos, and Cass couldn't think of a better way to ease the pain of doing hard time at Rancho de Fresas.

She read the note again. It said, *I liked* Planes, Trains, & Automobiles. *It made me think about loneliness and friendship and accepting others who are different. The scene in the airport with all the f-bombs hit the ears a little hard, but who hasn't been in a spot like that? We might not go berserk, but we sure feel like it. Anyway...I really liked it. Thanks for sharing. Now, I have something for you, and no, it's not a movie because there are plenty of great things to watch that aren't full of degenerate actors (smiley face). It's a documentary called* The Last Waltz, *by Martin Scorsese, and it's all cued up. I don't want to give anything away, so I'll just say it's sometimes difficult, and offensive, but mostly just plain beautiful. And there's music. Wouldn't it be great if we could describe everyone's life with these exact same words? Love, Micah.*

Cass liked the way Micah had described *Planes, Trains & Automobiles*: "...loneliness...friendship...accepting others." She felt those few words really captured the essence of it. And, of course, his signoff with the word *love* didn't escape her notice either. *What the hell*? she thought; at least the guy's not bashful. Besides, with the daily stress of the show and her uncertain struggles with Lenora, Cass felt like she could use a little uncomplicated love right about then. And who better to deliver it than an uncomplicated guy like Micah Bailey? But then she came to her senses and made do with a substitute that only a good movie, or, in this case, documentary could provide. She pulled the shades, grabbed the laptop, and curled up in bed. She wondered, would *The Last Waltz* be just as Micah had described?

Two wonderful hours later, she had her answer. *The Last Waltz* turned out to be one of those movies that in some small way had left Cass feeling like she'd become a better person just because she'd watched it. And yes, it was "sometimes difficult, and offensive, but mostly just plain beautiful" just as Micah had said. But to Cass, who loved movies of all types, the experience meant something more because in many ways it affirmed the convictions and the passions of her life, the same convictions and passions that *StarBash* attacked week after week. A friend had discovered a magnificent treasure and had shared it with her. And Hollywood—only Hollywood, with all its faults—was the conduit that had connected these two friends.

And if Micah wanted to argue that it wasn't a Hollywood movie, let him argue with the wind.

The next day Cass slipped into the workshop and left Audrey Hepburn and *My Fair Lady* sitting on Micah's desk. A few days after that, the laptop found its way back to her trailer along with a documentary called *Grizzly Man*, by Werner Herzog, which Cass found spellbinding, even if it did give her nightmares for a week. Sitting next to the laptop, Cass also found a key to the workshop. She countered with a key of her own, to her trailer, and *The Shawshank Redemption.* Micah responded with *In the Realms of the Unreal,* by Jessica Yu. That's when Cass realized that Micah had a great eye for movies. She also noticed that he hadn't balked when she dropped the pretense of recommending only movies that included a museum car. He watched what she recommended, and she did the same. *Maybe there might be hope for the Tinseltown terminator after all,* thought Cass.

In this manner, the two formed their own little movie club, which did wonders for Cass's sanity as she slogged through one *StarBash* week after another. Eventually winter turned into spring, miles and miles of ruby-red strawberries ripened on the gently rolling hills of Ventura County, and Cass almost believed that she might make it to the end of the ordeal.

CHAPTER NINE

On a rainy evening in April, near the end of the *StarBash* television season, Lenora sat at the desk in her home office and carefully inspected the mail. None of the letters had her name on them. They had Cassandra Moreaux's name. Lenora had been intercepting Cassandra's mail from the beginning. The effort hadn't produced anything of interest...until this day. Cassandra had received correspondence from a private investigator in Los Angeles.

The scalpel cut into the top of the seam on the ten-inch envelope and then sliced all the way to the bottom. In just a few seconds the envelope had been opened, and Lenora had the contents in her hand: a birth certificate and a printed summary of the detective's investigation. Lenora recognized the birth certificate. Three or four identical documents currently resided right there in her safe. She also recognized the names, dates, and facts in the report. Cassandra now had everything she needed. Time was running out.

Lenora had encountered formidable enemies in the past, but she'd never had one who marched as relentlessly as Cassandra Moreaux. And she'd never had one who's stated purpose had been to destroy the very thing that Lenora cared about most in the world.

Lenora didn't believe in self-sacrifice or any of the altruistic shackles that bound the human race. She had never known anyone who had turned ten bucks into twenty by turning the other cheek. She didn't believe in love, which she considered an affectation that desperate people add to compensate for emotional deficiencies. Even the idea of relationship, as practiced by the masses, baffled Lenora. She didn't understand why two people, who randomly converge at a place in time, felt the need to embellish the occurrence and call it something special. She called them affiliations and used them all the time. And when they lost their usefulness, she discarded them. Lenora understood self-sufficiency. She understood discipline, focus, and sacrifice. Most of all, Lenora understood the necessity of a person to change the world by living up to their full potential. And if that potential had enough power behind it, and if that person dramatically exceeded their potential by a wide enough margin, then that very same person had the rightful privilege of changing the world long after they had died. That's what Lenora believed in. She believed in legacy.

And what about existence itself, the philosopher's endless fodder? Lenora had come to have doubts about that, too. At best, even the most glorious existence represented a mere flicker in the infinite darkness...unless, once again, it had been properly illuminated by a carefully tended legacy. And Lenora had tended her legacy with meticulous devotion. And now the time had come to turn it loose. The final act of a perfectly lived life, Lenora believed, happened when the sheer glory and magnitude of the legacy fully supplanted the comparably weak and frail existence. Lenora looked forward to her final act, to the time when Lenora Danmore the person faded into the mist in order to make way for Lenora Danmore the young beauty who never ever fades. This eternal soul dances a ring around the world every day without fail. She sings and pouts and cracks jokes. The sun never sets without her laughing and crying with a million old friends. And when the sun comes up again, she makes a million new friends. Lenora had a vision of a perfectly lived life. Mortal must bow to immortal.

Lenora the decrepit must vanish so that Lenora the celluloid legacy could live forever.

But what happens when the celluloid legacy is threatened? In the past she'd had enough clout to easily squash it. She'd throw open a door, make the studio boss cry, and the next morning there'd be heads on silver platters. And now, decades later, Lenora no longer had any studio bosses in her pocket, but she didn't need them. She had the power of success and the passage of time on her side. Success smooths over blemishes, and the more success you have, the smoother you look. The passage of time works the same way. Events that happened sixty or seventy years ago seem to lose their girth. If you can see them at all, they look small compared to the problems of today. Even the so-called information age, in which the masses gorge on scandals of all sizes and shapes, had not harmed Lenora.

And yet one enemy still remained. This enemy had set her sights on the treasure of Lenora's life. That treasure included fifty-seven movies, seventeen top ten, seven top grossers, five Oscar nominations, and two best-actress wins. An unreasonable zealot had come to destroy a priceless legacy. Lenora's head popped with anger when she thought about it.

She put the certificate back into the envelope and resealed it. It didn't make any sense shredding it when the investigator had probably sent an electronic image before he even dropped this one into the mail. Besides, this problem had passed the point where papers, or even stacks of papers, even mattered. Nobody in the world cared about any of those papers...except Cassandra Moreaux. Cassandra had become the one and only problem.

The nightcap rested on a small tray that Micah held in one hand while he knocked on Lenora's door with the other.

"Put it on the coffee table," said Lenora from the office.

Micah pushed into the reception area and put the tray on the table. He poked his head into the office doorway. Lenora stared down at some envelopes on her desk.

"Good night, Lenora." said Micah.

"There's nothing good about it, Micah. Not until you make the deal for season five," said Lenora.

"Good night, Lenora. See you in the morning."

She didn't respond.

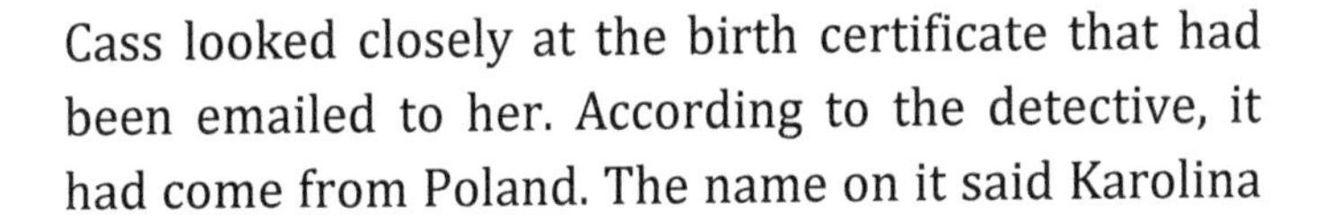

Cass looked closely at the birth certificate that had been emailed to her. According to the detective, it had come from Poland. The name on it said Karolina

Anna Wojtkowiak, which didn't look a whole lot like Carolyn Voyt, Lenora's supposed birth name. And that probably had been the key, just as Cass suspected. Lenora had a third name to hide behind. Lenora's betrayal of Cass's mom had never been found because Lenora had used a secret name, a name that she had kept safely buried in Poland for the last seventy years.

The detective also found another piece of the puzzle, one that Cass didn't know had been missing. As a matter of routine, the detective had investigated the parents, as listed on the birth certificate, and found that the father had been a known communist organizer who had fled with his family to America before the police could arrest him for suspected arson.

Cass immediately saw the significance. How much more likely is a person to snitch to the FBI if the FBI already has that person on the radar? And a Hollywood actor who happened to be the daughter of a known communist organizer certainly sounded like something the FBI would have found interesting.

This journey, a debt of love to her mother, had taken five long years. Wrong turns and dead ends had plagued her every step of the way. But now Cass started to believe that she might actually have Lenora cornered. Only one test remained: the name had to be sent to the FBI.

CHAPTER TEN

"And here's your *StarBash* host, the Tinseltown terminator himself, Micah Bailey!"

Cass watched closely. She'd heard rumors that on this episode the producers planned to milk every possible dollar out of the Cass and Brandi feud. The everyday booby traps had been bad enough. Now Cass had to deal with that. Micah flew through the hotel's giant revolving doors and bounded down the steps to the street in front. The exterior of the hotel had been partially reconstructed for his opening sequence. He stepped up onto a red-carpeted platform.

"Wow!" exclaimed Micah to the actors who stood around him. "Three months ago fifteen egomaniacs came to town. You had perfect hair plugs and enough Botox to inflate a football. And look at you now! The egomaniacs have almost become human, and there are only four of you left! That means one of you is about to become the owner of a little Greasy Dishrag that will change your life forever!"

The actors clapped, none more energetically than Brandi, and Cass realized for the first time just how badly Brandi wanted it. Her big mouth had destroyed her career, and now she hoped for an eleventh-hour reprieve from *StarBash*. Sad.

Micah continued, "In recognition of your achievement, each of you has been demoted to the Plaza Hotel concierge department. That's the good news. The bad news is that getting demoted means less money in your paycheck, which means you better shake the dust off your penny-pinching skills. But not to worry, my dear nouveau poor friends, we have brought in the reigning cheapskate champion of the world to help you do just that. His name is Elmer Stubhowzer, and Elmer recently took home the coveted Golden Coupon at this year's Cheapskate Championships held in St. Louis, Missouri. Please give Mr. Stubhowzer a warm *StarBash* welcome."

A middle-aged man dressed in purple polyester bellbottoms, a gold-colored shimmery button-down shirt, and platform shoes emerged from behind the crew and stepped up to the platform with Micah. His straight, long gray hair had obviously been the victim of many kitchen haircuts. Some kind of animal fang hung around his neck. He looked like a man serving a life sentence in a bad disco.

"Elmer, I understand that at the championship you turned $9.87 into two shopping carts full of food," said Micah.

"Yes, sir, that's what I did," said Elmer.

"That's impressive," said Micah. "Would you mind sharing some of your wisdom with the audience at home and with our starving actors here? I thought maybe you might pass on some tips to help them stretch a dollar the way you do."

Elmer posed awkwardly for one camera, then another, then back at the first, and said, "Well, I can't give away too many secrets, but a good way to start is to shop late at night and load up your cart with expiration dates. When you get to the register, tell them everything you got expires in thirty minutes, and you ain't got but a few dollars, and then offer five or ten cents on the dollar. Give that a try, and see if you don't turn a ten-dollar bill into food for a month." He smiled proudly, revealing a gold tooth that sparkled in the television lights.

Cass noticed a blue piece of tape stuck to the heel of one of his shoes. It looked like a garage-sale price tag. It said, "50¢."

Micah started to talk, but Elmer interrupted and said, "But the best way to stretch a dollar is to not spend no dollars at all. Like I said when they gimme the trophy in St. Louis, if you can make it or trade for it, why pay for it? Me and my wife Myra been livin' by those words since day one. Go ahead. Gimme the test. You name something, and I bet I can make it. Go ahead."

"Uh...OK," said Micah. "I wasn't expecting such an invigorating challenge, but...how about a...toothbrush?"

"Make it outta pig hair. Haven't paid for a toothbrush in forty years. Go ahead, gimme another one," said Elmer.

"Micah looked down at the carpeted platform and said, "OK, how about a throw rug for the living room?"

"Make it outta pig hair, just like the toothbrush," said Elmer confidently. "That stuff goes far. Rugs, fertilizer, toothbrushes, hairbrushes, paintbrushes are all made outta pig hair."

"Your pig must get cold at night," said Micah. "OK...you've got two strikes on me. How about a...a...refrigerator?"

"Don't need it. We pickle and can and salt everything we need," said Elmer.

"What about a car or a truck?"

"I got one of them. Traded two cows and my son Tommy for it."

"Um...Elmer, that doesn't sound completely legal," said Micah.

"Nah. Tommy don't mind," said Elmer. "Besides, the boys at the sawmill promised to trade him back when it comes time to castrate the sheep."

"Uh...OK...I guess since everybody seems to be happy with the arrangement, except maybe the sheep, maybe I better not judge," said Micah, with a pat on the champ's back. Then he continued, "Mr. Stubhowzer, it has been a pleasure talking cheapskate tactics with you, but I'm afraid the time has come for us to move on to the next part of our show. Would you do me the honor of helping with that?"

"Be my pleasure," said Elmer, who then pulled a piece of paper from his pants pocket and read out loud, "'Congratulations, actors. Each of you is now the personal concierge for the cheapest man in the world.'" He lowered the paper, flashed his gold tooth, and said, "That's me." He continued reading, "'You will be given a task. If you complete that task in the cheapest way possible, you will be demoted into the next round. If you don't, you will be fired.'"

"Thank you, Elmer," said Micah, who then turned to the actors and said, "By the way, for this contest you are being divided into two-person teams. One member of each team will be the concierge, and the other will be the assistant. You will choose a name for your team, and you will decide who gets to be the boss and who gets to be the assistant. At the end of the challenge, one of the teams will be eliminated. That means two of you will be going home instead of just one."

The actors groaned, and both of the Steadicams immediately zoomed in on Cass and Brandi. *And there you have it*, thought Cass; she and Brandi had just become partners, and *StarBash* just happened to have their cameras in the perfect position to start capturing all the fun. A production assistant immediately herded the two ladies together and escorted them to a cubicle that had been constructed in one of the soundstages. Cass also saw that for what it was: more *StarBash* bullshit; let's put the snarling animals together in a small cage and see what happens.

Cass entered first, followed by Brandi. The camera operator took a position in the doorway, backed by the production assistant. The cubicle contained a desk and two office chairs, one tucked behind the desk, the other placed in the corner of the cubicle. The chair behind the desk had the word "Concierge" nicely embroidered into the fabric on the back of the chair. The other chair had a piece of paper taped to it. On that paper someone had scribbled the word "Assistant." Cass saw a red envelope and a pen sitting on the desk. She reached for the envelope, but Brandi nudged her aside and got to it first. Brandi held up the envelope for the camera. *She's good at this shit. I need to get my act together*, thought Cass. Brandi opened the envelope and read aloud, "'We are having a picnic for three adults. I need ketchup, mustard, hotdog buns, hotdogs, relish, potato chips, and paper plates. And remember, there is no greater value than a great value that is valued greatly.'" Brandi dangled the letter for the camera and said, "I think we know who's most qualified to be the boss on this one."

"And who might that be?" asked Cass.

"The one who knows how to find a bargain because she been out of work thanks to a certain person who shall remain nameless."

"Yes, Brandi, you've got the market cornered on pain and suffering. We all know."

"You want a crack at it? Go ahead, but if you ask me, you couldn't win this one in a million years," said Brandi.

She's baiting me, thought Cass. But that didn't stop her from saying, "Fine. Give it to me."

Brandi held out the paper. Cass reached for it. Brandi took it back and said, "You can be the boss, Cass, but I'm not doing shit to help you. This one's on you. And I get to choose the team name." Brandi grabbed the pen from the desk, scribbled something on the paper, and handed it to Cass. It said, "Name of Team: Clueless."

As Cass scurried around in search of a cheap picnic, Brandi held court in the cubicle and trotted out a parade of snide remarks for the camera: "Too bad Bloomingdale's doesn't sell ketchup. If they did, Cass might actually have a chance"; "I'm worried about Cass. If she doesn't find organic, non-GMO mustard, I think she might have a nervous breakdown"; "Poor Cass. She googled 'cheap wieners' and got three hundred pages of porn."

Later that afternoon, with twenty minutes to go before the deadline, Cass entered the cubicle and proudly exclaimed, "I got ketchup and mustard packs for free and everything else at the dollar store. I think we won—no thanks to you."

"No, we didn't win. We lost. Congratulations. You completely lived up to your potential," said Brandi.

"What are you talking about? I paid five dollars for the whole picnic."

Brandi offered an angry, frustrated head shot to the camera—a pose she had been practicing earlier in the day—and said, "Come with me." She led Cass to a white passenger van that waited just outside the soundstage door. A second van containing crew and equipment idled behind the first. Brandi ushered Cass and the two-person camera crew into the van and then entered herself. Cass didn't think to ask how the crew and vans happened to be ready and waiting, a flub that made Brandi's plan a little easier.

The vans left the ranch and headed down the hill toward the city of Ventura. Cass shifted nervously a few times in her seat and after a few minutes asked where they were going. The great Casmo looked mousey. Brandi ignored her.

Twenty minutes later the vans pulled into a Walmart and parked. Brandi handed Cass a disguise that consisted of a wig and glasses. Cass looked at the bushy red wig and recoiled. Brandi held up another one and said, "I got one, too, so we're all even. Besides, you don't want your Hollywood pals to find out you shopped at Walmart, do you? They might kick you out of the club." Cass grabbed the wig and put it on. After this testy exchange, the tech guys fitted the ladies with concealed microphones and small transmitters. Brandi didn't want to attract a crowd, so she had instructed the crew to use concealed cameras and to keep their distance as much as possible.

Brandi led the charge into the store. She stopped just past the entrance to take in the scene—and to pose for the camera. Ah, the smell of America's favorite superstore, a simmering stew of popcorn, floor wax, and armpits that ran up your nose, shouting "Always Low Prices" every step of the way. Brandi liked it. She glanced at Cass, who stood next to her. Of course little Miss Nordstrom looked like she'd just been abandoned in a foreign country. This gave Brandi a really good idea. She turned to Cass and said, "You've been to Walmart before, right?" But before Cass had a chance to answer, Brandi did a mini arm flop for the cameras and said, "How come I'm not surprised? Well, let me give you some advice, missy. If you ever find yourself with five dollars in your pocket and a payday that's nowhere in sight, you might want to give this place a try. Not that that would ever happen to you."

"Brandi. Let me give *you* some advice," said Cass. "Stop wearing your sad story on your sleeve, and maybe you'll stop being such a miserable bitch."

"Wow. Something real from the Hollywood phony. I'm glad we got it on film," said Brandi. And then she marched away, straight to aisle five in the grocery department. Cass ran after her like a child who's afraid to lose her mother.

"What does this say?" asked Brandi, as she held up a bottle of ketchup and pointed to the label.

"Great Value," answered Cass.

Brandi put the bottle back on the shelf, moved down the aisle a few feet, and grabbed a jar of relish. "And what does this say?"

"Great Value," said Cass.

"That's right. That's the Walmart brand. Now read your instructions." Brandi whipped out the paper for everyone to see, and Cass started reading.

"'...And remember, there's no greater value than a great value that's valued greatly...' Oh shit," said Cass.

"Did you even bother to stop and think that maybe those strange words might mean something?" asked Brandi.

"I think we lost," said Cass.

"*We* didn't lose, Cass. I lost. You'll be going home to your Malibu mansion where you will live like a queen even if you never work another day in your life. I'll be going home to nothing. This was my last chance, and you took it from me, just like you did three years ago."

Cass stopped the camera crew at the door of the van and said, "Sorry, guys. No film on the drive back. Brandi and I have personal business to take care of. You'll have to hitch a ride in the other van." She climbed into the second-row bench seat, where the camera operator usually sat. Brandi sat in the next seat back. The van pulled away, and Cass turned to say something, but Brandi beat her to it.

"I don't know what you think you got planned here, Cass, but it ain't happening. You didn't talk to me when it really mattered. You sure as hell aren't talking to me now. Take your guilty conscience to a shrink."

"I don't have anything to feel guilty about, Brandi. I made a simple business decision, and for some reason you have decided to turn it into the defining moment of your life. That's the reason your career is stuck in the toilet, not because of anything I did," said Cass.

"You really don't get it, how all this works, do you? This might be reality TV, but that doesn't make it real. They pay me to say shit about you, so I say it. If you want the real truth, I'll give it to you now. I don't care about you, and I don't think about you. So don't flatter yourself," said Brandi, who then leaned back in the seat, put in some earbuds, and listened to music.

Five minutes later, as the van took the highway 33 turnoff toward the ranch, Brandi laughed out loud. Cass looked back at her. Brandi turned down the music and said, "You want to know the real joke? It's you and your self-righteous crusade against the blacklist. Maybe you should add your own name to the witch hunt."

"I didn't blacklist you," said Cass.

"Then where the hell have I been for the last three years?" yelled Brandi.

"You did that to yourself! You don't know when to keep your mouth shut! Lots of actors have opinions, but they know it's not smart to talk about it. Why do you have to be different?"

"Is that really your answer? If you got an opinion, keep your mouth shut, and we'll let you work? Are you listening to yourself?"

Cass had nothing else to say. She had tried, but the effort had been a complete waste of time.

Brandi and the other three actors retook the positions in front of the hotel that they'd occupied that morning. Micah stood before them on the platform, getting ready to film the last segment of the second-to-last show of the season. Brandi had been the one to beat all season long, having won twice as many competitions as the next closest competitor. Even now, some sixteen weeks later, she felt focused and alert and planned to stay that way until she got what she came for.

The cameras rolled, and Micah said, "Two of you are going home, and two of you will be demoted into the final round where you will battle it out for the *StarBash* Greasy Dishrag and a ten-million-dollar movie deal. Are you ready to learn your fates?"

The actors leaned forward and clapped nervously, except Cass, who apparently had too much dignity to care about such things.

"Very good," said Micah. "But before we do, let's invite back our special guest, Mr. Elmer Stubhowzer. I understand he has some parting gifts that he wants to pass out to our contestants. Come on up here, Elmer."

StarBash liked to pump up the excitement, pop it in the actors' faces, and then pump it back up again during the last few minutes of the show. It kind of made sense. They had a forty-three-minute time slot and had to fill it with something. Normally Brandi knew better than to get too excited the first time Micah got excited, but maybe this week her focus had been just a little too sharp. She took a deep breath and watched Elmer, the redneck penny-pincher, bounce up to the stage and stand next to Micah. He wore the same gold-toothed smile and thrift-store duds from earlier in the day. He also carried a large burlap bag.

"Hello, Elmer. What do you have in the bag?" asked Micah.

"I got stuff for the actors," said Elmer.

"That's great. I'm sure our actors appreciate that. I'll step aside, and you go ahead and do your thing, my friend."

Elmer reached into the bag and pulled out what looked like a bundle of thin leather straps that had things dangling from them. He separated one of the straps from the others and held it up for the camera. It was a leather necklace with a large animal tooth.

"That's nice," said Micah. "What's it made of?"

"A pig's tooth."

"Yes, of course it is. It was silly of me to even ask," said Micah.

One of the Steadicams followed Elmer as he placed a necklace around the neck of each actor. Brandi fingered the menacing fang and smiled. She actually liked this sort of thing.

When he'd finished, Micah said, "Very good. What else do you have for our lucky contestants?"

"I saved the best for last," said Elmer, as he pulled a large mason jar from the burlap bag. It contained a yellowish, fleshy substance suspended in liquid. He held it up to the camera and said, "It's my famous pickled pigs' feet that won fifth prize at the Butte County Fair!"

"Elmer, I have to ask you a question about your pig," said Micah. "Do you ever get the feeling that maybe he's doing more than his fair share of the work?"

Elmer considered the question for a few seconds and said, "No, can't say as I do on account of it being a pig and all. That's what pigs do. Now if it was a rightful member of the family, then maybe you might have a point."

"Then that's good enough for me, my good man," said Micah. "You go right ahead and pass out what's left of your pig."

Micah watched Elmer hand a jar to each of the contestants and then said, "Very good, Mr. Stubhowzer. Is that everything?"

"Yes, I believe it is, except for the payment. They each owe me thirty dollars—twenty for the necklace and ten for the pig's feet."

Micah looked confused, and so did the actors. Brandi didn't have any money on her, and probably neither did anyone else. It had to be a joke. After a few awkward moments, Micah said, "Never fear, my friends; this one is on *StarBash*. No expense is too great when it comes to an actor's rehabilitation." He pulled out a small wad of cash and said, "How much do I owe you, Elmer?"

"One hundred twenty dollars."

Elmer held out his hand, and Micah peeled off six twenty-dollar bills. But Elmer kept his hand out and said, "Plus three dollars California sales tax." Micah counted out three dollars.

"And forty cents California bottle deposit," said Elmer.

Micah gave him another dollar.

"And one dollar California grocery-bag fee for the reusable grocery bag," said Elmer, as he held up the burlap bag.

Micah looked at Elmer and said, "I think you'd make a good lawyer. Have you ever considered that line of work?"

"Yes, sir, I did at one time," said Elmer. "But then I realized I had a reputation to keep, so I let it go."

"That's a good point. Besides you are really good at what you do," said Micah, as he added another dollar to the heap. The two men then shook hands, and Elmer left with a pocketful of money and a spring in his step.

Micah turned to the actors and said, "All right, that was fun, but now it's time to get down to business." An assistant relieved the actors of their little piggy treasures and Micah continued: "In this battle, Team Tightwad took on Team Clueless in the great American picnic challenge, where you had to buy a picnic worthy of the cheapskate champion of the world. But we're not talking about just any old cheap picnic; it had to be a *Great Value* picnic."

Out of the corner of her eye, Brandi saw Cass shift nervously and look at the ground.

"Tiffany! Please bring me the envelope," said Micah.

Tiffany and all her curves slinked past the cameras. She handed the envelope to Micah and slinked away. The actors held hands. Micah tore open one corner of the envelope and paused. He said, "Have any of you ever been this close to ten million dollars in your entire life?"

The actors moaned.

Micah tore open the rest of the envelope and pulled out the card. The actors closed their eyes. Micah said, "And the team advancing to our final round, where they will compete against each other for the coveted Greasy Dishrag, is...Team Clueless!"

Team Tightwad groaned, Cass gasped loudly, and Brandi smiled confidently.

"Wow!" said Micah. "Such different reactions! Cass looks completely shocked, and Brandi looks completely confident. Ladies, come up here and tell our audience what's going on."

They stepped up to the platform and stood next to Micah, one on each side.

"Let's start with you, Cassandra. Why the surprise?"

"Uh...uh...to tell the truth, I'm a little confused...because I thought I had bought the wrong things," said Cass.

"No, you didn't," said Micah. "Everything you purchased had the Great Value logo on it. How do you explain that?"

"I can't," said Cass.

"What about you, Brandi? Cass says she bought the wrong stuff, but now it's the right stuff. Can you explain it?"

"Yeah, it's easy," said Brandi. "Cass didn't have a clue, so I filled my own bag and switched it with hers when she turned her back."

"Um...you belong to the same team. Wouldn't it have been easier to just tell her?" asked Micah.

"Some people you can talk to, and some you can't, so let's just say I'm glad the whole thing is over," said Brandi.

"And now the two of you will be going head-to-head for ten million dollars," said Micah. "Do you care to make a prediction?"

"I'm gonna kick her ass. That's my prediction," said Brandi.

"I imagine you have an opinion about that, Cassandra. Do you care to share it with us?" asked Micah.

"I'm going to do my best, and it's going to be a lot of fun," said Cass.

What a dummy, thought Brandi. Micah had given Cass a chance to take a jab, but of course she had to play it like Sister Grace-Be-with-Thee.

It had been a very great day for Brandi. She had served a batch of hot, stinky humility to her enemy, and she had made it to the finale. She'd actually made it. And the best news of all? She'd be going up against Cassandra Moreaux, the ultimate Hollywood puppet. Cass knew how to follow the herd. She knew how to smile, and bat her eyes, and tap dance her way out of a jam. She didn't know *StarBash*, and she especially didn't know the *StarBash* audience. Brandi knew these people. She understood them. In many ways she was one of them. And, besides all these advantages, Brandi still had a weapon that Cass would never have, the weapon that had helped her to make it to the end: she had the power of revenge.

She started using it that very night.

After they'd wrapped for the evening, Brandi handed Cass a folded newspaper and said, "This hits the stores tomorrow, but I got an early copy especially for you. I hope you enjoy reading it as much as I enjoyed writing it. Plus, they paid me ten thousand dollars. Isn't show business wonderful!"

When Brandi thrust the rolled-up newspaper into her hand, Cass didn't look at it. Why give her the satisfaction? Besides, the smile on that chubby face said it all: more bad news had just arrived. When she got back to the trailer, Cass found out exactly how bad. It was a supermarket tabloid, and the front page showed a series of pictures of her and Micah. One of the pictures showed Micah coming out of Cass's trailer. Another one showed Cass unlocking Micah's door. The final picture showed one of the notes Micah had left for Cass. It included the word "love." In screaming red letters the headline said, "Casmo Sleeps with the Enemy!" Splashy bullet points under the headline said: "A-Lister Goes Bonkers! Career is Toast! Ditched by Hollywood Pals!"

CHAPTER ELEVEN

The changing of the seasons in California just doesn't seem to pack the same punch as in other parts of the country. But for Micah it did...for at least one of the seasons anyway. It happened when the *StarBash* season ended and anything but *StarBash* began. And with another show in the can, and only one more to go, the fresh scent of a new season had started blowing through the ranch.

His spirits had been lifted for another reason, too. Even though the show had gotten hopelessly sidetracked over the years, for the first time, he liked where they had ended up. He liked Brandi, and he liked Cass. Though they had completely different personalities, they both had a core of decency that guided their lives, and they had lifted the show with that decency.

On this night, just after wrapping for the week, he had popped over to the workshop to grab his mail. As he started to open the door, headlights flooded the building, and a familiar car pulled up. It was Cass, in her black BMW. She lowered the window and said, "Remember when you invited me to dinner?"

"Yes," said Micah.

"Good. I accept. Get in."

"Uh...OK," said Micah. He got into the car.

Cass had on the same peach-colored cashmere sweater and designer jeans that she'd worn earlier on set. She said, "Buckle up," and then stomped on the gas pedal.

"I take it you're hungry," said Micah.

"You have nothing to smile about, Micah. This isn't a date. It's a distraction."

"OK. A good distraction is probably better than a bad date, so I'm down for that. What exactly am I distracting you from?"

"See, you're already doing a good job. Maybe this won't turn out to be a terrible decision after all," said Cass.

She then tossed a newspaper onto his lap. Micah looked it over and thought of a few jokes but then saw Cass's clenched jaw.

"I'll give you one guess who did it," said Cass.

"I'm hoping Lenora did it because then that would mean you got off easy with whatever deal you have going on," said Micah.

"Good guess but wrong answer. Brandi did it."

"I'm sorry, Cass. You don't deserve this."

"Has anyone ever told you that you're obsessed with Lenora?"

This blunt question surprised Micah, but he chalked it up to Cass's disturbed state of mind. He answered, "Yes. One person has said that."

"Your wife?" asked Cass.

"You know, I'm probably only good for one distraction," said Micah. "Are you sure this is the one you want?"

"I'll make a deal with you," said Cass. "You tell me about your marriage, and I'll tell you about mine, and then we'll both be miserable. And if you make your marriage more rotten than mine, I'll even pay for dinner. How's that sound? But first tell me where we're going, and the more crowded the better. My career is scorched, so we might as well make a big splash and give these idiots something decent to gossip about—besides this bullshit."

Micah gave her directions to the restaurant, and then his brain scrambled to think of the words to describe his marriage. He never talked about it. And since he never talked about it, he had zero confidence in his ability to choose words that had even a hint of presentable gloss to them. So over the next twenty minutes, as they made their way down the hill, Micah gave Cass the unglossed version of a short marriage that had ended four years earlier. It hadn't been a rotten marriage. It had been a crowded marriage, and Micah had had the power to make it uncrowded, but he didn't do it. And it hadn't been a case of meddling. Lenora, the unwelcomed third party, hadn't cared enough to meddle; after four years living under the same roof, she barely knew Heather's name. It had been crowded by Micah's devotion to Lenora, devotion that had rightfully belonged to his wife. At first he'd convinced Heather that he just had a demanding job, like millions of other people. It didn't take long, though, for her to see through that. And then she eventually left, and Micah didn't stop her.

"Why didn't you fix it? What does Lenora have over you?" asked Cass.

"It's not her. It's me. It's like she's a math problem, and I'm the only one in the world who can solve it. And if I give up, the answer will be lost forever."

"But maybe, if you lose the answer, you'll find out that life is better without it," said Cass.

"There's no maybe about it," said Micah, "but here I am, still at the ranch with Lenora."

After this the two fell silent for a while before Cass said, "Uh...does this mean it's my turn?"

"Yes, I believe that's what it means."

"Any chance of a rain check?"

"Yeah, I suppose so, but only because I'm the distractor, and you're the distractee, and everyone knows the distractee isn't required to say a word."

"I like this game," said Cass. "Are you ready for the next question?"

Micah said yes but secretly hoped that the next question would be easier than the first.

"Why did you ask me out?" asked Cass.

"That's an easy one. You're not afraid of people, and I find that interesting. I've seen it. You rush into the mess without giving it a second thought. You're not afraid of the sadness or the ugliness, and because of that, you find beauty that would otherwise be lost. Who knows, maybe I'm hoping some of it will rub off on me."

Cell phones immediately popped into the air from tables and booths all around. Cass had grown accustomed to the phones and the clicking and the excited whispers of the picture takers, even if it did sometimes get tiresome. On this night Cass barely noticed. She had other things on her mind. She had problems. And now, before they had barely made it to the restaurant, Cass had added a new one to the pile: She liked Micah Bailey, and the more she got to know him, the more she liked him. Cass had officially crossed over to the dark side.

She especially didn't need this kind of problem. The Micah Bailey problem didn't synchronize with her other problems. In fact, it made them even worse: "Hi. My name's Cass. I'm reading for the part of Betty...oh, don't mind him. He's with me, and he hates Hollywood..."

She thought about putting on the brakes, reining in her feelings, or at least burying them in a hole for a few weeks until the dust had settled from the demolition of her career, but Micah's straight-shooting ways completely disarmed her. One minute she had the menu in hand and talked pleasantly about peanut coleslaw, in full control of her faculties; the next minute she found herself blabbing about her train-wreck marriage in glaring black-and-white honesty. Cassandra Moreaux just didn't do things like that. It was scary confessional kind of shit. She told it from beginning to end, about two top-of-the-world fun-loving actors who got married and moved straight into the Hotel Hollywood power suite. About how she thought she had lucked out with a dream marriage that made all of her friends envious. Whenever one of the tabloids did a marriage issue, they put Cass and her husband on the rock-solid, smiley-face side of the page. Until one day they didn't anymore, and Cass found out that she had married a cheater who had started cheating before they had even gotten home from the honeymoon.

At some point, when telling the tale of a bad marriage, a common practice is to recount some of the good times and then gracefully segue into platitudes about busy lives and best friends who drifted apart but who will still be friends forever. Cass didn't do that. She told Micah about the crushing humiliation and despair that had plunged her into a pit with no bottom. She also admitted that she had loved her career more than she had ever loved her husband, and he had known it. So in a sense, she had been a cheater, too—just not quite in the same league.

On several occasions Micah opened little exit doors in the conversation to give Cass the opportunity to quit. Cass ignored them. She told Micah the whole truth. She told him things that you only tell a mother—or a guy with a cardigan sweater and a fancy degree hanging on the wall. That's the kind of power Micah had over her.

Up until the very end, the night had been great. It had started out as a selfish distraction for Cass, and it turned into an unexpected human connection. And who knew what else it might have eventually turned into. But then one of those difficult life-lesson moments popped up, and it happened to be a lesson that Cass hadn't yet learned. That night the lesson sank in but only after the damage had been done.

She learned that there's a certain responsibility attached to the kind of raw honesty that she and Micah had shared. It's a responsibility, a trust really, that both parties will protect the deeply personal vulnerabilities that make that kind of honesty possible in the first place. Unfortunately, Cass and her temper violated that trust in the worst way.

The problem started after one of the servers came up to their table and said, "Please forgive me, Miss Moreaux; I don't mean to be rude, but I have to tell you that when you went on that show, I got really pissed—uh...no offense, Mr. Bailey." Micah smiled graciously, and the server continued: "I felt like you had sold us out...actors, that is...but after the way you stood up for us in the bar a few weeks ago, I changed my mind. We actually have someone to fight for us now. I'm proud of what you're doing, and I'm proud to be an actor. OK, that's it. I just had to tell you."

She started to leave, but Cass quickly grabbed her hand and said, "Can I ask your name?"

"Almita Deleone."

"Can I ask you a question, Almita?"

"Yes," said Almita, nervously.

"What do you think about the feud between me and Brandi?"

"Truthfully, I hope you guys become friends. I know Brandi says things that get her into trouble, but I still hope you become friends. This business is hard enough anyway. Why make it harder with stuff like that?"

"Thank you, Almita. You've been very helpful." After Almita left, Cass turned to Micah and said, "The only problem is Brandi won't talk to me."

"How come?" asked Micah.

"I don't know…she thinks I blacklisted her."

"Why does she think that?" asked Micah.

"Because she went ape-shit political a few years ago, and I refused to work with her," said Cass.

"And she got fired," said Micah.

"Yes."

Micah looked down at the dessert menu, and Cass wondered if it might not be more of an evasive maneuver than an interest in a hot-fudge brownie. "So what do you think?" asked Cass.

"I think it happened a long time ago, and what's done is done," said Micah.

"OK…it happened a long time ago. Now tell me what you think."

"Cass, you've had a rough day. Why not talk about this later?"

"All right, now you're starting to make me mad," said Cass.

"OK. I'm just wondering what you would have done if you had liked her politics."

"Nobody likes her politics! She's a terrorist with two sticks of dynamite up her ass! And I stood up to her. I stood up for what is right."

"The substance of Brandi's politics has absolutely nothing to do with the question of a blacklist," said Micah. "What matters is whether or not she got punished because of those politics. Look at Joseph McCarthy. He fought against communism, and that's not such a bad thing, but he still got it completely wrong."

"Are you comparing me to Joseph McCarthy?" asked Cass.

"You're missing the point," said Micah.

"Obviously. What exactly *is* your point?"

"I'll say it again. What would you have done if you had liked her politics?" asked Micah.

Cass didn't say anything, but it didn't matter because they both knew the answer.

In a calm, quiet voice Micah said, "That's the essence of a blacklist. Someone doesn't believe what we want them to believe so we take away their job. And when it comes from someone with power, the results can be devastating. I'm sorry, Cass, but if I didn't tell you the truth, what kind of friend would I be?"

"Yeah, well, you and truth have a funny kind of relationship, Micah. The only truth you're interested in is the kind that fits into a narrow little box. Everything else is a lie! And let me ask you this. Where exactly does all the *StarBash* bullshit fit into this truthful world of yours? Every week you tell fifty million people that actors are less than human and deserve to be treated like shit! Did it ever occur to you that just maybe we are nothing more than the people from your beloved Main Street, USA? We're good and bad, strong and weak, rich and poor. But for some reason you've decided that we don't fit into that perfect little box of yours!"

"Yes, you might be from Main Street, but not all of Main Street is welcome in Hollywood. That's one of the main points of the show. But you're right, Cass. That whole bit is off base. I was trying to be funny. I thought it was just a joke."

"That's the problem. You're so caught up in your little mommy complex and your hatred for Lenora, you can't tell the difference between what's funny and what's not." Before these stinging words had left Cass's mouth, she knew she had gone too far.

Micah's face turned red, and he said, "I'm not your enemy, Cass. We might not always agree, but I'm not your enemy." Then he got up and left and never came back.

CHAPTER TWELVE

Micah slouched in a chair by the bay window in Lenora's front parlor. He stared at a half-full tumbler of whiskey that rested on the coffee table next to him. He didn't feel sociable, but he didn't feel like drinking alone, either. He needed mindless, chirping bodies who knew how to keep their distance. Lenora and her actor friends filled the bill. They sat at a card table across the room.

"What's with the Boy Scout and the booze?" asked one of the ladies in a whisper that Micah easily heard.

"I don't know. Maybe he's working on his single-malt merit badge," said Lenora.

The ladies laughed. Micah looked up. They looked down at their cards.

None of the ladies came close to Lenora's stature. And neither had any of the others that had been a part of the group over the years. Lenora carefully chose the planets that orbited her star. And if they didn't properly reflect her glory, they got the boot.

Micah also chose his friends carefully. He didn't like sharp tongues. It had been an acquired preference, developed over the last twenty-five years while he worked with the sharpest tongue in Hollywood. He liked debate and sarcasm and repartee because those activities possessed an innate forward-looking quality to them; like a great rally in tennis, you keep hoping the next verbal shot will make it over the net and the rally will continue. When words are respectfully used in this manner, issues can be settled, and great ideas can be cultivated. When words are used as weapons, on the other hand, everything stops, and all that's left is a crater. Ironically, on several occasions Micah had seen Cass purposefully moderate her speech when many others in the same situation would have resorted to verbal carpet-bombing. It had been one of the things he liked about Cass. Now he didn't know what to think.

His own actions with Cass that night also confused him. He'd never been the type to bail over a few ruffled feathers. He and Lenora used to stand toe to toe for twenty or thirty minutes at a time. While everyone else on set had died at the mere sight of their historic confrontations, Micah treated it like just another day at the office. Obviously, Cass had hit a sore spot on him.

"You know, Lenora, if you get bored with your toy, I wouldn't mind borrowing him for a while," said one of the ladies.

"Take him, please, but I have to warn you, he's got a mouth on him," said Lenora.

"I don't mind. Jerome hasn't said a word in ten years. It would be a nice change."

Micah downed the drink and poured himself another.

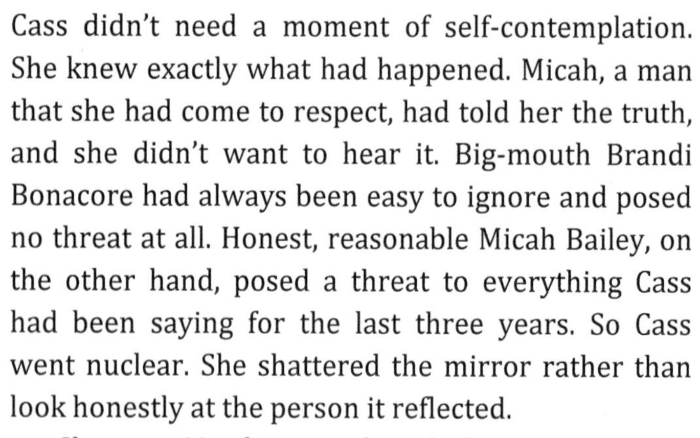

Cass didn't need a moment of self-contemplation. She knew exactly what had happened. Micah, a man that she had come to respect, had told her the truth, and she didn't want to hear it. Big-mouth Brandi Bonacore had always been easy to ignore and posed no threat at all. Honest, reasonable Micah Bailey, on the other hand, posed a threat to everything Cass had been saying for the last three years. So Cass went nuclear. She shattered the mirror rather than look honestly at the person it reflected.

She sent Micah an apology before even leaving the restaurant. He answered right back but not in the way she had hoped he would. He asked a simple question about the argument that had led up to her cruel outburst but didn't say a word about the outburst itself. Then he signed off with a lukewarm cliché about friendship. He didn't reveal any resentment or hurt feelings. If anything, the message had the sound of a Dear Jane letter to it, like Micah had taken a step back. Cass couldn't say that she blamed him.

And the question he asked, gentle as usual, hit home like a warhead. He said, "You obviously love Hollywood very much, which means you want only the best for it. Let me ask you this question: Will Hollywood be a better place if people like Brandi are banned from participation?"

As soon as Cass read the question, three words popped into her head: *whole human experience.* And she knew the answer. It all boiled down to those three words, words that represented the noblest contribution that Hollywood had ever or would ever make to the world: its relentless pursuit of the whole human experience. Like painting the Golden Gate Bridge, the pursuit of this prize never ended because the human experience never stopped changing, but that didn't matter in the least. The pursuit itself was the prize. And it belonged to everyone, paid out every time we went to the movies and got carried away because we saw some part of ourselves in that movie. And the reason we saw ourselves was because we are part of the human experience that Hollywood had faithfully captured and added to its dynamic catalog. Hollywood also benefited from this endeavor because it meant that instead of just a handful of potential stories to tell, it had millions, including the story of you, of me, and of the villager half a world away who lived a fascinating existence that would never be shared if not for Hollywood's honorable passion.

But how could Hollywood ever hope to capture the whole human experience if it pretended that vast segments of the human experience didn't even exist? Such myopic exclusion didn't amount to anything "whole." It amounted to a skewed sampling that insidiously chipped away, little by little, at the humanity that made movies so magical. If left uncorrected, eventually every production ran the risk of at least a slight taint, not necessarily because of malice but simply because it had been generated from a system that had replaced the whole human experience with an ideological imposter. The results might be artistic but wouldn't be pure, just as propaganda can be artistic but will always be tilted in a way that favors ideology over purity.

Cass saw it clearer than ever. Hollywood needed the Brandi Bonacores of the world. It needed Walter the prickly bar manager and Elmer the backwoods skinflint. It needed sophisticates and potato farmers, intellectuals and factory workers, bog hoppers and subway riders. It needed everyone.

Unfortunately, this sanitary, philosophical revelation contained an ugly omission that now stared at Cass like a mugger: it didn't address the very gritty issue of her guilt, a guilt about which she no longer had any doubt. She had destroyed Brandi's life. And she had done it just because she didn't like what Brandi believed. This knowledge hit Cass like a slug in the gut. She didn't know where to even begin coming to terms with it.

It had been a difficult last few days and much of the difficulty had been of Cass's own making. She had honestly begun to wonder if she even still had the ability to make a single right decision.

Micah stood unsteadily at the door and knocked. Lenora answered from the other side and told him to put the tray on the coffee table. Micah wobbled forward and deposited it in its usual spot, but not before spilling half the drink. He giggled and wiped away the evidence. The sound of Lenora pounding away on her computer keyboard echoed from the nearby office. Focused, determined, and always pounding. Unless she got interrupted. Micah poked his head into the doorway and called out her name.

She didn't answer. He called her name again. This time she said, "What?"

"Please pardon my phraseology," slurred Micah, "but will you kindly tell me exactly what floats your boat? And please keep it short as I do not believe I shall be standing in the very near future. Thank you."

Lenora's head slumped forward, and she let out a frustrated sigh. She swiveled around, removed her reading glasses, and said, "This is what happens when you drink too much."

"Specifa...specifa...specifically, I need to know what you care about...besides the museum," said Micah.

"I see," said Lenora, with a frown. She continued: "Micah, if you waste all your time thinking about the things you can't have, you'll never get the things you can have. You're a successful man. Isn't that worth something to you?"

"Thank you. I've been told that a successful man is better than an unsuccessful man but nevertheless, madam, I do not believe you have answered the question," said Micah with a prosecutorial flourish.

"You know the answer," said Lenora. "It has never changed, and it never will. I care about my next project. And the one after that. And the one after that. Everything else is a distraction."

"Even a successful man?" asked Micah.

Lenora looked Micah dead in the eyes and said, "It depends on whether he's part of the project or not."

"I rest my case, Your Honor," said Micah. He then navigated his way out of the spinning room.

The next morning Micah informed Lenora that *StarBash* had finished its run; there would not be a season five because he planned to kill it. Lenora simply shrugged and said that maybe Micah had been right all along. With the opening of the museum, maybe it didn't make sense to spread themselves too thin. Then she told him that she had booked him a flight to Florida to check out the 1926 Hudson from *The Grapes of Wrath*, if he didn't mind.

The Hudson sounded great...until he thought about it for maybe one second. Since when did Lenora care at all about the car museum? And when did she ever, in all her regimented discipline, leave money on the table? The ratings for *StarBash* still hadn't peaked. That cow still had piles of cash left in her, and Lenora had just shrugged. And, finally, why hadn't she exploded and let loose with the famous ranting, threatening Lenora Danmore diatribe? The whole conversation didn't make sense.

CHAPTER THIRTEEN

On Tuesday morning, June 3, the day before the *StarBash* grand finale, the intercom buzzed in Lenora's office on the second floor of the museum. The voice in the box informed Lenora that the guard at the front gate had detained a private detective who said he had an appointment to see Cassandra Moreaux.

Lenora had been expecting something like this. She said, "Let him pass."

She then took the elevator down to a special exhibit. While the presence of a private detective snooping around the ranch might not have sounded like the best news, it had at least given Lenora a warning and an opportunity to select the battleground where the first skirmish with Cassandra Moreaux would soon play out.

After a visit that lasted less than five minutes, Cass said goodbye to the detective, closed the trailer door, and stared at the envelope he had left behind. It said, *Federal Bureau of Investigation, Record/Information Dissemination Section*. The detective had already seen the contents of the envelope and had insisted on hand delivering them to her. He didn't feel comfortable mailing them and especially not emailing them.

Cass had been in this spot three times before, and it had always ended with failure and a dead end. She told herself not to let the detective's ominous behavior get her hopes up, but it didn't work. This time had to be different, she just knew it. She pulled the contents from the envelope and found a copy of her original FOIA request along with a case report from 1952 that included copies of an original, handwritten form and two pages of typed notes. This was definitely different from the other times. This was something. It looked like Cass had finally figured out the secret password: Karolina Anna Wojtkowiak.

She eased into the swivel chair by the front door and began reading.

While Lenora waited, she surveyed the progress on her latest interactive creation. A single overhead work light illuminated the set, which stood about half-complete. The clipboard in her hand contained a long fix-it list for the crew that would be in later that day. Lenora quickly scribbled out another item for the list. The emergency exit, which she had purposely left ajar, suddenly opened, and bright light spilled into the exhibit. A dark silhouette flowed in with the floating particles of dust and light. The door closed, the blinding light subsided, and the silhouette gained an identity. It was Cassandra Moreaux, right on time.

"You lied to me, Lenora. You lied to my mother. And you've been lying to the world for seventy years," said Cassandra.

Lenora had successfully beaten down these dreary accusations more times than she cared to remember. She'd had a perfect game plan, a perfect playbook, and a perfect record. But now the game had changed. Cassandra's threat represented more than just another armchair sleuth or a gossip columnist trying to beat a deadline. She possessed intelligence and determination. Most dangerous of all, she had the scorched-earth mentality of a daughter out for vengeance. Lenora reached into a nearby utility box and turned on the main circuit breaker. This powered up the entire exhibit, including lighting in the viewing area. Lenora looked at Cassandra and said, "Yes, dear, I do lie—that's what happens when you associate with lawyers—do you care to tell me which lie you might be referring to?"

"Don't you dare try to get clever!" shouted Cassandra, as she charged into the viewing area. The ladies now stood just feet apart, separated by the low partition that divided the viewing area from the set. Cassandra said, "Shut your mouth, and listen! Listen to the words of a coward and a traitor!" She read from some papers that she clutched in her hand. "'Subject requests immunity from prosecution. Subject requests anonymous cooperation. Subject requests limited ID verification and personal disclosure limited to parts 1A, 1C, 1D. In exchange for the above, subject agrees to anonymous surrender of document containing evidence of communist subversion within Hollywood community.'"

The speech ended and gave way to a menacing glare. Lenora said, "All right. What do you want me to say?"

"These aren't the words of a desperate suspect who's been backed against the wall. I could almost forgive you for that," said Cassandra. She held up the paper and picked out a few of the words, "'...anonymous cooperation...anonymous surrender...limited ID verification...' Those are the words of a negotiator who has something to sell. You coldly negotiated the sacrifice of another human being. You stabbed my mother in the back, and you had it planned out right down to the untraceable name you used!"

Lenora carefully eyed Cassandra. Everything rested on Lenora's next move, but the timing had to be perfect. She silently waited a moment longer. Cassandra spoke.

"You get one chance to tell the truth, Lenora, and you don't even deserve that. Tell me why you did it."

"I wanted to work, so I chose the side that would let me do it," said Lenora.

"And did you know that you were next in line for the part in *Monty's Revenge*?"

"That wasn't the reason—"

"Did you know?"

"Yes, I knew."

"I'm calling a press conference," said Cassandra. "And after the story I tell, you will be dissected right down to your rotten core. You are going to die in disgrace, Lenora. This pathetic shrine is going to crumble, and you will be remembered as the ruthless coward that you truly are." Cassandra turned and left.

Lenora removed the lanyard from around her neck. It held her museum ID card. She reached over the partition and dropped the card into the illuminated circle on the floor. The set lighting instantly popped on. It buzzed vibrantly. A young woman dressed in a chorus-girl costume appeared from the wings. She had long legs, rosy cheeks, and a cute blonde ponytail. A bright spotlight followed along as she walked to the center of the exhibit. It was Lenora's most recent android creation, a creation that Cassandra knew very well. Lenora said, "Cassandra, before you go, I think you might like to see this."

Cassandra turned around. Lenora watched carefully. Cassandra gasped. Her stony face melted into a mess of forlorn sentimentality. She slowly walked back to the edge of the viewing area and braced herself against the partition. She said, "Why did you do this, Lenora? Why did you do it?"

Lenora said, "Listen to me, Cassandra. I don't want to fight anymore. I want to surrender, but I knew you would never listen to me. I knew I had to prove my contrition. And this is how I'm going to do it."

Cassandra jabbed at the flowing tears and said, "I don't believe you."

"This exhibit is dedicated to your mother. Will you let me tell you about it?"

"Can she talk?" asked Cassandra.

"She will when we're finished...plus a whole lot more than that."

Cassandra said nothing. She stared at her mother and shook with emotion.

Lenora continued, "It's from *Zombies on Broadway*, in the diner, where your mother steals the carnation from the lapel of the mean aristocrat. It was her best movie. Manny Farber said your mother 'singlehandedly turned matinee fodder into a must-see event,' and Hedda Hopper listed her as one of the year's top newcomers."

Cassandra fought for composure. After a moment she managed to blurt, "This doesn't change anything."

"I haven't told you the best part," said Lenora. "We've also recreated the entire basement scene in Zander McCreery's theater, including the dance."

The tears now ran more than ever, undeterred by any degree of dabbing or wiping.

"I...I don't believe it...Not from you...I don't believe you..." blubbered Cass.

Now the time had come to make the move. Lenora spoke in a quiet, defeated voice. She said, "When you first started closing in, I only saw the scandal and the death of my museum. Of course I searched for one last lie that might save it, like I had always done, but it didn't work. You loved your mother too much, and that gave you a determination that I couldn't beat. That's when I gave up, but it's also when I realized that the museum didn't need to be saved at all. It had the strength within itself to rise up from the rubble of my guilt and be something beautiful. I just had to let it go. I had to hand it to your mother and let her take it to a place that I can't go. That's when I started working on Wendy Rainy and *Zombies on Broadway*."

At that moment a door in Cassandra's heart opened just a crack. Lenora saw it in her eyes. Lenora continued, this time with a pinch more passion: "I might have to be banished, but that doesn't mean the museum can't go on. Instead of only one actor, it can be a tribute to all actors. These days our dirty laundry is hawked on a million different websites, but who is telling the story that really matters? Who is showing the world the vital role that actors play in our world? That's what this museum can do! And your mother is the perfect one to lead the charge! She is the very face of the hardworking actor, and nobody deserves to be showcased more than she does. All I ask is that you give me a few days to prepare the transition, just until the grand opening, where we will scale back the exhibits, and your mother will be the only star on the playbill. I will round up top-tier investors from around the world, and Wendy Rainy will show them exactly what this museum can be. And then I will be gone. I just need your blessing to do it. I need you to let your mother shine."

CHAPTER FOURTEEN

Brandi felt her heart pounding all the way up into her neck. She wanted it too badly, and that was the best way to screw the pooch. It didn't help that the final show filmed in front of a live audience and that she'd be in the spotlight for almost the entire time. She closed her eyes and started another round of breathing exercises. After a few minutes, Cass joined her in the left wings as they waited for their cue. They'd been dressed in perky pink-and-white waitress outfits and had caught glimpses of the set—the interior of a diner—so they had a pretty good idea that the final challenge had something to do with waiting tables. That worked perfectly for Brandi. She'd waited tables for years when breaking into the business and had gone back to it in the last year after hitting the skids. She didn't know if the great Casmo had ever stooped that low, but it didn't matter; no way in hell was that Hollywood powderpuff going to outhustle Brandi—unless Brandi didn't get the jitters under control. She breathed in deeply through her nose and exhaled very slowly out of her mouth.

Cass wanted to say something, anything, even if it amounted only to some kind of olive branch, but Brandi had busied herself with her preshow routine. On top of that, her body language had clearly put out a "Cass not welcome" sign.

And not only Brandi wore that sign that day; when Cass ran into Micah backstage, he brushed past her with nothing but a curt hello.

Cass knew better than to expect an easy fix to the problems she had created. She had, however, hoped to at least make a start of it—especially with Brandi, the one who Cass had injured most seriously.

But now Cass had no choice but to try to clear her head and concentrate on other things—like fixing her life. *StarBash* had ruined it, and as pathetic as it sounded, *StarBash* had the power to fix it. That's what winning this final competition meant. Four months earlier Cass had entertained notions of destroying this little tyrant TV show. Now the tyrant had a boot on her neck, and Cass had been reduced to begging for her life. It was sad but not as sad as limping away with a second-place trophy and a reputation as the idiot actor who had flushed her life down the toilet. She had to win this thing.

The house lights dimmed, the theme song swelled, and the curtain opened...to a completely empty stage except for an old man who stood behind a very large steel sink. He wore a wet, dirty apron over a threadbare T-shirt and black work pants. Gray stubble blurred the boundaries of his face. His short gray hair looked matted and recently slept on. The inside of his right forearm had a tattoo. Cass couldn't tell for sure, but it might've been an anchor or a crucifix.

A pile of dirty dishes towered above his head on one side of the sink. An island of dirty foam floated on top of the water in the sink. The man stared down at it. He reached into the water with one hand and pulled out a dishrag. He held it up to the light, looked at it, and tossed it to the floor. It landed with a soggy *splat*. He reached in again, fished around for a few seconds, and pulled out another rag. After some examination this rag also ended up on the floor. When the third try ended the same way, he grabbed a bucket from under the sink, turned it upside down, and stood on it. He wobbled, steadied himself, and from this elevated position reached deep into the giant sink with both arms. He fished around like before but didn't find anything. He reached in farther, so that half his shoulders disappeared from view. His chin dipped into the foam, but with a great deal of effort, he managed to keep the rest of his head dry by craning it backward. Soon, however, he gave this up and lowered his entire head into the water as well. The audience gasped. Displaced foam and brown dishwater spilled onto the floor. The man's upper torso sank down the hole next, and then his midsection. People squirmed. A smattering of hushed whispers rippled through the assembly. Now only his legs and feet remained. They stuck straight up into the air, moving and wriggling but not giving the impression of distress. Then, like a stricken ship succumbing to its fate, his remaining limbs disappeared into the water. The stage went black, and an anxious murmur took hold of the audience.

This *StarBash* spectacle had only just begun, however, as Cass soon found out. A fierce howling wind rose up out of nowhere, shook the walls, and then gave way to an even louder screeching groan that seemed to come from the roof, as if the fierce gale had just torn the top off the building. Cass peeked through an opening in the wings. Through the dim emergency lighting, she saw part of the first row of seats. The people in those seats sat rigidly straight with wide eyes. A bolt of lightning suddenly pierced the blackness, followed by a deafening clap of thunder, and those people started screaming—along with every other soul around. The lightning bolt had hit the big metal sink head-on, violently throwing it a foot off the ground. A second booming lightning bolt assaulted the sink again, and even louder screams erupted. After a third bolt hit the sink, when the audience seemed to be on the brink of hysteria, the storm ceased, and a single spotlight popped on and offered just enough light to restore some degree of calmness. The spotlight focused on the sink, which made a hissing noise and billowed big clouds of steam. The sink's metal legs glowed red, first weakly, but the glow quickly spread and deepened into a succession of hotter shades of fire. As the glow intensified, so did the hissing and billowing. The sink glowed and hissed and billowed, loudly, dangerously, like a runaway reactor. And when the end came, when one thermal degree too many had been added to the inferno, the resulting explosion elicited the kind of frenzy that would have been the envy of any amusement park in the world. Sometimes you scream for fun. Sometimes you scream because you're scared shitless. This sounded like the scared-shitless variety.

Fortunately, the beleaguered audience had a surprise waiting on the other side of all that terror—if they dared to open their eyes: an arm had risen up out of the sink, and it clinched a purple dishrag in its fist. The Greasy Dishrag had arrived. For the *StarBash* faithful, the importance of this moment roughly amounted to the arrival of the Olympic torch—or maybe even the Ten Commandments. They rose as one, clapped wildly, and the orchestra played a majestic tune. *These people know how to put on a show*, thought Cass, begrudgingly.

Now the time had come to see who owned the arm that had fearlessly delivered the beloved icon, a.k.a. time for Micah's big entrance.

The audience retook their seats and watched expectantly as the arm—and the body to which it belonged—magically rose from the sink, straight up into the air. After the arm, a big fluffy chef's hat rose next out of the abyss...because everyone knows the best way to get promoted from dishwasher to chef is to get regurgitated out the business end of a dirty sink. The mystery man under the hat faced backward, away from the audience, but the short neat haircut looked suspiciously familiar. A white chef's neckerchief followed. And if you have a chef's neckerchief and a chef's hat, you better also have a chef's coat with contrasting black Mandarin-style collar and long sleeves with contrasting black cuffs. And such broad, athletic shoulders, too. Who could be so dashing? And who could be so dry?—he didn't have a drop of water on him. Could it be the Tinseltown tomato?

And then he moved—whoever he might be. He tucked the dishrag into his coat pocket and extended both arms straight out to the side, like a diver on a diving board.

"And here's your *StarBash* host, the Tinseltown terminator himself, Micah Bailey!" boomed the announcer's voice.

The mystery man, arms still extended, flexed his legs, sprang into the air, and performed a perfect backflip that landed center stage in front of the sink. The instant he landed, the set exploded into a pyrotechnic volcano that showered the entire stage with fire and sparks and smoke. The awestruck audience jumped to their feet again and let loose with a torrent of screams, whistles, and applause. And when the conflagration onstage ended with an extra burst of fire, and after the smoke had cleared, they discovered that the dreary, empty stage had been miraculously transformed into a vibrant, glistening 1970s-style diner that included bright-yellow Formica countertops, a row of gaudy orange booths, and a shiny red-and-white checkerboard floor.

And the terminator himself, dressed in his chef's outfit, stood in the middle of it, facing the audience, beaming like a triumphant magician. *And who could blame him*, thought Cass. It looked really fun.

Micah soaked up the applause for a few seconds and then threw up his arms and said, "Wow!"

The audience yelled, "Wow!"

"I said wow!" repeated Micah.

"I said wow!" exclaimed the audience.

During this exchange a gold towel rack resting on a black-and-white marble pedestal descended from above and gently landed next to where Micah stood. Micah removed the purple towel from his pocket and reverently draped it over the rack. He then turned to the audience and said, "Hello, America! Welcome to *StarBash*, and welcome to our 2020 grand finale! Tonight this little dishrag is going to change someone's life forever! But before we get to that, let's take a look at the incredible journey of our two fearless semifinalists." The dishrag ascended back into the heavens, and a prerecorded video played for the audience. It basically amounted to a greatest-hits collection of Cass and Brandi's many catfights.

Cass knew that the clip lasted a few minutes, so she had time to try again. She touched Brandi on the arm and said, "We may never see each other again, Brandi, so I just want to say that you were right; it wasn't fair what I did, and I'm sorry, and I hope someday I can make it up to you...if you will let me..." She extended her hand.

"Good try, Cass. Those kind of mind games don't work with me," said Brandi.

And right at that moment, as if to highlight their estrangement, the film clip showed the scene where Brandi blew the torn-up paper into Cass's face. *That pretty much says it all,* thought Cass. The anger and resentment had too tight of a grip. At this point Cass didn't know what else could be done.

The segment ended, and Micah said, "Put your hands together and welcome your *StarBash* grand finale contestants, Cassandra Moreaux and Brandi Bonacore!"

Cass turned on a big smile and waved to the crowd as she and Brandi found their spots on a little strip of stage in front of the set. Micah stood next to them, and they all faced the audience. A row of booths, followed by a counter with barstools, lined the stage behind them. Behind the counter aisle stood a wall with a kitchen pass-through that included heat lamps, an order wheel, and a stainless-steel counter. Ashtrays, napkin holders, ketchup bottles, chrome menu holders, salt and pepper shakers, and little table tents with pictures of apple pie occupied their appropriate places throughout the diner.

"Entertainment is a trillion-dollar business!" exclaimed Micah. "It's the opium of the people, and Hollywood is our drug dealer. And sometimes I think it's time to give the dealer the boot and for us all to go to rehab. I make no apologies for feeling that way."

The audience clapped. They knew the routine: Micah bashes Hollywood, and they cheer. And, this being the last show of the season, Cass expected that

Micah might want to have more fun than usual. She was right.

Micah pointed to Cass and Brandi and said, "And here, my friends, we have the drug itself. These are the pretty faces that fuel our hallucinations. They are the afternoon tea with laudanum that makes us feel good about our prospects for love and happiness. They are the hypnotic voices that delude us into believing that good always triumphs over evil. They are Doc Hollywood's miracle tonic, and we love it more than any junkie ever loved his drug."

And the Tinseltown terror is off and running, thought Cass. *Time to buckle up—and to stay alert—* because Micah had completely jumped the rails; the teleprompter had his lines cued up, but he had galloped off in a completely different direction. *Oh well. Just another fun day on* StarBash. She stood picturesquely and smiled like a good little reality-TV star.

"But are they human?" yelled Micah.

Some in the audience yelled back: "No!" Micah began pacing back and forth. One of the producers, who sat in the front row with his family, looked around nervously.

"Are they human?" yelled Micah, louder, with wide, crazy eyes.

This time no one said a word. Complete silence blanketed the soundstage. Cass heard the director's screams from Micah's earpiece. Micah removed the earpiece. Cass cleared her throat to get his attention. He threw her a quick, cold stare. Now Cass got seriously concerned. Micah looked like he had more than show business on his mind. He looked agitated, like a guy with blood on his shirt and a head full of rambling, angry words. The possibility that he might say those words to fifty million people with her standing next to him smiling like an idiot did nothing to ease the apprehension. She wondered if Lenora and *StarBash* and all the negativity had finally cracked open his sanity. She wondered if her cutting jab at the restaurant had had anything to do with it.

Micah stopped pacing and faced the audience. "Are they human?" he screamed, with clinched jaw and bulging veins.

"Yes" came a quiet, solitary voice from somewhere in the audience.

"Yes!" exclaimed Micah. "Yes! They are human! And the only thing inhuman around here is the idea that someone is disqualified from the human race because they are weak or imperfect. Or because they have a different opinion. That's exactly what we're supposed to be fighting against!" He looked down for a few seconds and then said, "But somehow I got things turned upside down, and that needs to get fixed. Will you help me do it?"

The audience responded tepidly.

"I'm asking you to help me," said Micah.

This time they responded with a bit more energy, but, honestly, Cass didn't think she had ever seen a more confused audience. It didn't seem to bother Micah, though. He took a spot next to Cass and Brandi and picked up the teleprompter right where he had left off. Thankfully, that quickly led to a commercial break. Micah turned to Cass and Brandi and said, "Sorry about that little detour. I had some housekeeping to take care of." Then he brushed past the frazzled director, who had charged up to the stage to confront his erratic star, and went down to visit with the audience. He shook hands, signed autographs, and posed for selfies. He worked the crowd like a pro. The Hollywood basher had more Hollywood in him than he cared to admit, a glaring fact that everyone seemed to know except Mr. Tinseltown himself.

After the break ended, Micah retook the stage, the cameras rolled, and he had the audience right back in his pocket. He said, "Congratulations, ladies. You have been demoted. Caviar crepes at the Plaza Hotel are now a distant memory. Today you are slinging hash in Bart's Diner, and the next step for one of you is the Greasy Dishrag." He turned to Brandi, who stood on his left, and said, "Tell me, Brandi, who's going to be doing the dishes at the end of the night?"

"Me! Take a look at these," she held up her hands. "These dishpan hands haven't seen a nail salon in thirty years."

"Very impressive," said Micah. "Now tell me one more thing. You've suffered some setbacks in your career. What do you say to the young woman who's about to hop a bus to come chase her Hollywood dream?"

"I say go for it! Get on that bus! But when you get here, you better keep track of who you are and what you believe, or you're gonna end up being just another Hollywood clone...like some people we know."

"OK..." said Micah. He then turned to the other side and said, "Cassandra, your opponent is clearly holding a grudge, but you haven't said much about it. This is the last show. Do you think now might be a good time to share your side of the story?"

"No. All I can say is that I have apologized to Brandi, and I hope someday we can move forward, but right now she isn't really interested."

Brandi stepped around Micah, glared at Cass, and said, "That's bullshit, Cass. If the person who blacklisted your mother came up on this stage right now and apologized, would that be good enough for you?"

These words caught Cass completely off guard. The plight of her mother had always been Cass's own private battleground, and no one had the right to trample through it...except for someone who had been hurt just like her mother. And now Brandi seemed to think that that included her. Cass honestly didn't see anything in common between what happened to Brandi and what happened to her mom. But, up until a few days ago, Cass hadn't been able to see her own guilt, either. Did she still have her head partly buried in the sand because she didn't want to admit that she'd been just as guilty as Lenora Danmore? And that her pursuit of Lenora had been an epic hypocrite's crusade? And did she really want to talk about any of this shit on national TV? But the question had been asked in front of millions of witnesses, so she had to come up with something. She refocused, fumbled for some words, and then Brandi beat her to the punch, once again. She said, "No! It wouldn't be good enough because that kind of apology is like an icepick in the ear! So you can just save it, Cass. I never want to hear it again."

"As you can see, ladies and gentlemen," said Micah, uncomfortably, "this truly is a grudge match, and now we have no choice but to turn the enemies loose." He pointed stage right of where he stood and said, "Ladies, please step to the side and prepare to face your challenge." Cass and Brandi stepped aside, and six men entered from the opposite side of the stage. They wore identical yellow T-shirts that included a design that showed the initials *BLE* sandwiched between two hamburger buns. Beneath the hamburger graphic, the shirts said, "Big League Eaters of America." The men formed two rows, facing Micah, stage left of where he stood. Micah pointed to the first man in line and said, "Please state your name and occupation."

"My name is Joey Pickman, and I am the number-one-ranked Big League Eater in the world."

"Welcome, Joey. Please tell our audience what you did to earn that title."

"I ate seventy-four hot dogs in ten minutes."

The *StarBash* crowd liked this kind of thing. They clapped for the guy like he had perfected nuclear fusion.

The five remaining men introduced themselves and recounted their digestive conquests. They all then took seats in the diner.

Micah turned to Cass and Brandi and said, "Ladies, these are some big eaters. Each of them can devour a hot dog on a bun in ten seconds, and they can do it fifty or sixty times without breaking a sweat. Today they are at Bart's for a light snack—thirty hot dogs and a beverage—and your challenge is to serve it to them. You have each been assigned three customers, one per table. In order to win the challenge, you must be the first to complete the following tasks." Micah pointed to the menu on the wall above the kitchen pass-through, which had transformed into a big electronic scoreboard. It listed Cass's name on one side, Brandi's on the other, and all of the tasks in the middle. Micah read the tasks from the scoreboard. He said, "You must: 'Take the orders'; 'Serve the meals'; 'Clear and clean the tables'; 'Collect six dollars in tips'; and 'Ring the bell' by the cash register." As he read off each task, bright red check marks appeared under each woman's name next to the corresponding task. Micah continued: "If you fail to complete any of these tasks, you will lose the challenge. Pencils and order pads are in your apron pockets. Bar towels and bus trays are behind the counter. Brandi will carry only blue plates, and Cassandra will carry only red plates. Now we will clear the scoreboard, and you will step over here next to the counter and line up behind the red line."

Cass lined up first, facing the kitchen pass-through where she'd be collecting the plates of hot dogs. Brandi lined up next, but she faced the opposite direction, toward the booths where the customers sat, and held her order book in her hand like a baton. Cass quickly fumbled for her order book and switched directions. The audience laughed. She'd never waited a table in her life, a fact that was now rather obvious.

"Oh. I forgot to tell you," said Micah. "It's one hot dog per plate, so that means you will be carrying ninety dinner plates...plus three beverages...moving as fast as is humanly possible." He smiled. Brandi smiled. Cass cussed under her breath.

Micah turned to the audience and said, "Are you ready to see someone do the dishes?" The audience rose to their feet again. "Are you ready to hand out a little pocket change?" They stomped and cheered. A giant check for $10 million, held by Tiffany Talador, appeared from the wings. Besides pointing at things, Tiffany also carried big checks. She passed once in front of the audience. Micah reached behind the counter and pulled out a big gun. If this was supposed to be a starter pistol, then they had gotten it from the *Dirty Harry* track-and-field catalog. Micah pointed it into the air and said, "On your mark! Get set!" He fired the gun.

Cass thought that she had formulated a decent plan—shadow the more experienced Brandi, copy her every move, and then slip into the lead at the very end—but it pretty much fell apart before the gun smoke cleared. Brandi just moved too fast. She had all three orders pinned to the wheel before Cass had scribbled out her second order. Next came the drinks, and Brandi confidently held the tray above her shoulder and shot from table to table. Cass carried the tray like a third grader with an egg on a spoon. The worst part came when Micah, their cook for the evening, started throwing plates of hot dogs onto the pass-through counter. Brandi hauled ten plates at a time, lined up and down both arms like some kind of greasy-spoon contortionist. Cass carried four at a time and dropped the whole load once when she got distracted by the sight of one of the men stuffing an entire hot dog down his throat.

These guys really did devour a hot dog and a bun in ten seconds, and the audience went completely nuts over it. And Brandi almost kept up with them. Every time she showed up with a big load of hotdogs, the crowd cheered, and the Big League Eaters treated everyone to an up-close demonstration of their gastronomic talents. And then Cass showed up with a measly four hot dogs, and the audience groaned. Brandi's three customers hammed it up and put on a great show. Cass's customers twiddled their thumbs.

A loud horn blew, and a red checkmark flashed onto the scoreboard every time Cass or Brandi completed a task. Within just a few minutes, Brandi had three checkmarks, and Cass had one. And whenever Brandi got a checkmark, she stopped, faced the audience, and yelled, "Now we're cooking with peanut oil!" Cass figured that it had to be some kind of redneck joke. Whatever it was, the audience loved it.

The plan obviously had been a failure, but Cass didn't panic. If she knew anything about *StarBash*, she knew that drama always waited just around the corner. And sure enough, when things looked their bleakest, a little bit of drama rolled up and hit her right in the foot.

After Brandi's customers had left, while she wiped down one of her tables, the bar towel accidently swiped a coin off the table. Brandi didn't see it and, thanks to the noisy audience, didn't hear it either. The coin hit a barstool on the other side of the aisle, rolled back across the aisle, and hit Cass in the foot just as she reached a customer with another round of hot dogs. Cass calmly deposited the dinner plates onto the table and reached down and plucked the quarter off the floor.

A few seconds later, Brandi slammed her fist down onto the bell by the cash register. The audience cheered, and she launched into one of her honky-tonk victory dances—seasoned with extra peanut oil. Cass looked up at the scoreboard. Brandi had all five checkmarks, but one of them flashed on and off, presumably because it needed to be verified. Nobody knew it, but that wasn't going to happen. By the time Cass had collected her tips—all quarters—and hit the bell, Brandi had expanded her celebration down to the front row of the audience. Cass looked again at the scoreboard. Just like Brandi, she had all the checkmarks, and one of them flashed on and off. There happened to be one important difference, though: Cass had six dollars in her pocket, and Brandi didn't.

Micah pushed through the swinging door, cruised through the restaurant, and took the same spot in front of the set where they had started. Cass joined him. Brandi gyrated her way up to the stage and wedged herself in between Cass and Micah. Cass obliged and moved over a step. Micah wore a huge smile, bigger than the usual game-show host, and Cass wondered why. Had he been secretly rooting for Brandi all along? It made sense. In Micah's world, Brandi Bonacore qualified as the perfect star for a lavish anti-Hollywood production. She had bravely challenged the evil empire. She had been driven to the brink of annihilation. And now she had a happy ending that included a triumphant ride back into the chastised town for some good old-fashioned bootlicking and crow eating.

Sometimes, though, the real ending isn't the happy one.

The stage lights dimmed, and the orchestra played a somber, ceremonious tune. The audience quieted. Micah removed his hat. The marble pedestal that held the beloved icon descended from on high, escorted by spotlight and accompanied by the man-eating dish sink that had recently been the source of so much handwringing. A gold box, about half the size of a breadbox, now rested on the pedestal next to the towel rack. The box looked like any other square, gilded container except that it had a large funnel-shaped bowl attached to the top, presumably to collect whatever the box stored. When the ensemble landed on the stage, the spotlight that had accompanied the journey expanded to include everyone onstage.

As the orchestra continued in the background, Micah said, "Brandi, before we turn you loose on this dirty old sink, there is some housekeeping to take care of. Are you willing to trade six dollars in tips for a Greasy Dishrag?"

"You bet your ass," said Brandi.

Micah pointed to the gold box and said, "Please deposit your tips into the coin counter."

Brandi scooped the coins out of her apron pocket and plunked them into the funnel on top of the box. The sound of jostling coins and a whirring machine echoed through the soundstage. The growing tally flashed onto the scoreboard as the coins rolled down the funnel and into the coin counter. The tally stopped at five dollars and seventy-five cents. Micah hesitated. He cleared his throat. He said, "You...uh...seem to be a little short."

The audience laughed.

Brandi smiled, felt around her pocket, and said, "No, that's all of it."

Micah looked down the funnel end of the box. He pulled out a small drawer from back of the box and looked inside where the drawer had been. He then emptied the coins from the drawer into his hand, reinserted the drawer, and counted the coins by placing them in one-dollar stacks onto the pedestal.

One of the stacks came up short. Micah said, "I'm sorry, Brandi. You are missing a quarter."

Brandi's hand shot back into the pocket. The outline of her fingers could be seen digging from corner to corner. She pulled out the order book and shook it. Nothing shook loose. "No. That's it. I got it all. I swear that's all there was."

"No, Brandi. There was a total of six dollars left on your tables, and that has been verified by the judges."

"No, I'm telling you, I got it all. That's all there was," said Brandi. Her wisecracking smile had turned stiff and plaintive.

The orchestra stopped playing.

"I'm sorry, Brandi, the rules are very clear," said Micah. "If you can't complete the task, Cassandra Moreaux will be given the opportunity."

The audience gasped.

"It has to be back on one of the tables," said Brandi. She turned toward the booths.

"No," said Micah. "There's no going back. If you can't find the missing coin, you must step aside."

Now the tears began streaming down Brandi's cheeks. A few minutes ago, those plump, rosy cheeks had been wreaths of glory. Now despair had left them twisted and ugly. Her body shook as it fought back the convulsion that precedes an impending sob. Her arms twitched. Her left hand dug compulsively into the empty apron pocket.

Cass looked at Micah. He also looked devastated, and Cass understood it perfectly. Most of his dogmatic bluster boiled down to two simple words: right and wrong. He believed in them like a Boy Scout. Others might argue about his particular interpretation of right and wrong, but no one argued about his conviction. The same held true with the way Micah handled conflict. He put an unusual amount of effort into treating people fairly. Cass had experienced it personally and had witnessed it countless other times. She had no doubt that in Micah's eyes the prize belonged to Brandi because it was right, and it was fair. And now a meaningless technicality had upset his perfectly ordered apple cart.

Cass believed in right and wrong, too. If you have a love affair with Hollywood, right and wrong will always be along for the ride because virtually every movie ever made there revolved around some interpretation of those two words. And even now, on a disgusting little reality show, those two enemies had locked horns once again. Cass believed in right and wrong, but how much did she believe? Did she believe enough to sacrifice herself? Did she believe like Micah believed? Yes, she did. She knew it without reservation. It had taken three long years, and an unpleasant detour, but the truth had finally broken all the way through.

Cass reached into her pocket and pinched a quarter between her fingers. She then locked hands with Brandi. Brandi shot her a hateful glare and tried to pull away. Cass held tight. She then pressed the coin into Brandi's palm and said, "Brandi, things don't just disappear. It has to be stuck in your order book. Why don't you look one more time?"

The audience clapped. Brandi's glare dissolved back into sadness. She bit her lip, and the tears flowed more than ever. Cass pressed hard on the coin and said, "Please, Brandi. No one deserves it as much as you. Don't give up. It has to be there."

Brandi closed her hand around the coin, and Cass released her grip. Brandi once again shook the order book. This time a coin plonked onto the floor, rolled across the stage, and hit Cass in the foot. The audience rose to their feet and clapped. Cass looked down at her foot. *This damn coin is giving me a headache*, she thought. She picked it up, looked at Brandi, and said, "May I?"

Brandi couldn't speak. She nodded.

Cass dropped the coin into the funnel, and the tally hit six dollars. Flash bombs exploded, confetti rained, and, in typical over-the-top *StarBash* fashion, all hell broke loose.

Brandi grabbed Cass into the most powerful Italian bear hug that anyone had ever lived to tell about. Cass heard the sobs. She felt the shudders. And then she heard Brandi say, "I should have accepted your apology because now I know you really meant it. I'm sorry; I should have forgiven you."

And then she grabbed the Greasy Dishrag and twirled it over her head like a stripper. Brandi had made it back, and Hollywood was a better place for it. Hollywood was a better place, and Cass had helped to make it happen. It was a good day.

CHAPTER FIFTEEN

Before the last piece of confetti had barely hit the floor, while Brandi stood in front of a hundred reporters and ten thousand camera flashes, while the rest of the cast—from first show to last—ramped up the wrap party, Micah dashed up the hill from the soundstage to his workshop. He needed to look at something.

From his desk he logged into the online film vault and found the footage from the master shot camera for that night's show. A staple of television, this camera used a wide angle to capture all the action and all the players from the beginning of the show to the end. He loaded the footage into the computer program and hopscotched to the part where Brandi found the missing coin. From there it took about ten seconds for his suspicions to be confirmed: Cass had rescued Brandi.

Micah leaned back in his seat and shook his head. Almost anyone can be selfless if they have enough time to think about it and to arrange the circumstances so that the unpleasant act will cause as little discomfort as possible. Cass hadn't had any of that. She'd had mere seconds to decide. She had a large sum of money at stake. Her fans wanted her to win. Her career desperately needed a win. Fifty million viewers had the reasonable expectation that she herself wanted to win. Yet, under the bright lights, under the weight of all those expectations, instead of winning she chose to help another human being. Cass Moreaux had done it once again.

And this was the same Cass Moreaux whom he had just ditched.

Micah had to wonder about his defective powers of discernment. He valued a thoughtful, steady demeanor over many other qualities, but his appraisal of Cass had been all over the map. First, before he had even met her, based on nothing but her Hollywood address, he decided that she had to be just another rotten apple. Then he got to know her, corrected his evaluation, and got it right. Then she lost her temper, he stormed off like a child, and he plopped her back over to the other side. Now he had video proof that he had been completely wrong and had to put her back where she should have been all along. He had been wrong, right, wrong, and right. He either needed to get his act together or go on medication.

In the meantime, while he sorted out these personal issues, the question of what to do next waited to be answered. While the heart clearly knew what it wanted, the head had some serious questions to ask. Namely, if the heart actually got what it wanted, what happened next? Life at the ranch? The same ranch that had killed his marriage? Life in Hollywood? Micah didn't even want to think about that. And, thankfully, he didn't have to because he didn't have time to think about anything. Starting right then, the next twenty-four hours of his life had been booked solid with interviews and other *StarBash* promotion. And immediately after that, Lenora had saddled him with museum business on the other side of the country.

If the ranch never gave him anything else, it always gave him a safe wall of obligations to hide behind. Success breeds obligations, and more success always means more obligations. And at the ranch you ground through them because nothing ever got in the way of success. As Micah sat at his desk and thought about these things, his eyes fell upon the picture of his wife. She looked peaceful, like a day at the beach. For some reason the sight of that image, which depicted perfect contentment, began to distort the sight of the obligations that had been spawned from his latest success. They changed shape. They looked less like the by-product of success and more like feeble excuses that felt uncomfortably familiar. They tugged on his sleeve and said, "She's leaving. What are you going to do about it?" They whispered in his ear and said, "Here we go again." They made him wonder why he found it so difficult to draw a line in the sand.

CHAPTER SIXTEEN

Micah woke up the next morning in a bad mood. He'd finished the first round of network interviews at two in the morning and had tried to catch a few hours of sleep. Thoughts of Cassandra Moreaux got in the way. Now he had to meet up with Brandi for a full day of interviews in Los Angeles and then catch a red-eye to Florida.

To make things worse, he also suspected that Lenora had a new scheme stewing in the cauldron. For her the cars had always been an afterthought—second fiddle to the real star of the show—and she didn't trouble with them. But now, with a mountain of work still to be done on the rest of the museum, she had suddenly become interested, going so far as to personally book his flight to look at a car. It had to be a Lenora scheme. But was it an everyday pain-in-the-butt scheme, or was it a lock-the-doors-and-call-the-lawyer kind of scheme? In the end Micah decided to just get the trip over with as quickly as possible. The ranch would be virtually empty because the show had ended and the museum staff would be going home for the weekend. He'd hop over and hop right back. How much trouble could she get into in just two days?

He threw some clothes into a suitcase and headed out the door.

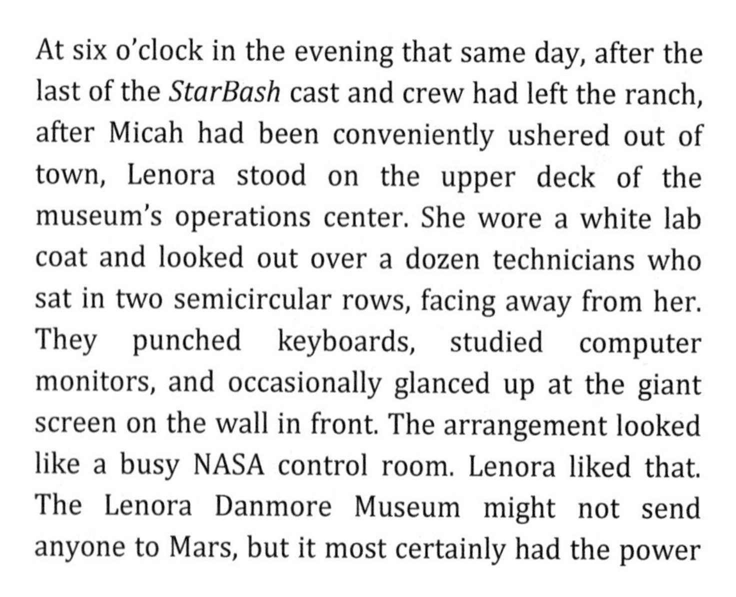

At six o'clock in the evening that same day, after the last of the *StarBash* cast and crew had left the ranch, after Micah had been conveniently ushered out of town, Lenora stood on the upper deck of the museum's operations center. She wore a white lab coat and looked out over a dozen technicians who sat in two semicircular rows, facing away from her. They punched keyboards, studied computer monitors, and occasionally glanced up at the giant screen on the wall in front. The arrangement looked like a busy NASA control room. Lenora liked that. The Lenora Danmore Museum might not send anyone to Mars, but it most certainly had the power to open up other worlds for all who dared to step into her footprints.

"Listen up, people. It's going to get busy, and you must stay in character at all times," said Lenora. The technicians swiveled in their chairs and looked back at her. "And don't be afraid of a few glitches. We call them hiccups...or brain freezes...or senior moments. It's part of being human. If one of your cast members has a deviation, you are to follow low-level protocol. If that resolves the issue, send them to their next cue. If it doesn't, send them to the shop and grab one of your backups. You are not to power down under any circumstances. This will be just a short test. If everyone does their job, you will be on your way home for the weekend in less than an hour." Lenora's team of wonks then swiveled back around and resumed their work.

The giant screen on the wall showed a live shot of the circular drive in front of the museum. A red carpet lined the walkway from the curb to the opened museum entryway doors. Limousines, luxury cars, and a smattering of requisite eco cars waited in line for the red carpet. These shiny vehicles carried a large variety of android cannon fodder—presented as nondescript, rich investors—because a grand opening with only one guest wouldn't fool anyone. It also gave the crew a chance to warm up before the main event. Lenora carefully observed that warm-up now.

A limousine pulled up to the red carpet. Uniformed valets opened the car doors, and the fashionable occupants emerged, he in tails and she in a shimmering evening gown, their perfectly believable human images gently kissed by a thousand camera flashes as they walked an invigorating gauntlet of photographers. These guests then rendezvoused with the ubiquitous velvet-voiced, microphone-wielding, red-carpet MC. He'd been programmed for wit and charm, and to lob sycophantic questions about beauty and prestige to the VIP guests. This type of personal interaction carried inherent risk, but the scene required it. Besides, even the most human of humans looked plastic in these particular affairs, so Lenora felt confident that her plastic MC would be safe. She had put her best technician on it just the same. At the end of the carpet a small cadre of snappy servants stood at the ready with champagne, hors d'oeuvres, and a pleasant escort into the exhibit.

Lenora liked what she saw, but it really didn't matter. Turning back wasn't an option. The job had to be done that day.

When the black BMW pulled up to the curb, Lenora resisted the urge to rally the troops. In case anybody ever asked, they had to be able to say that it had been just another day at work.

Cassandra exited the car. She wore a little black dress with pearls and a skinny smile. She looked tense if not a little suspicious. Lenora had expected something along those lines.

"And here's Cassandra Moreaux, one of Hollywood's hottest actors right now, thanks to her impressive showing on *StarBash*," said the MC, as Cass passed through the gallery of photographers. "Let's see if she has time for a few words." He pointed the microphone at his target, waited for her to enter the kill zone, and said, "Cassandra, are the rumors true that you and Brandi Bonacore are in negotiations to do a movie together?"

Cassandra studied the MC closely for a few seconds and then said, "What a beautiful voice you have. I don't recall ever hearing it before. What's your name?"

"Rallye Rollins, BBC London, and thank you very much. That's a compliment I'll cherish forever."

Cassandra removed a phone from her black handbag, punched at the keys for a few seconds, and then looked up at Rallye. She had obviously searched his name. Clever. But not clever enough. Rallye Rollins had a website, social media presence, and an unflattering online DUI mugshot.

"Yes, that's right." said Cass. "Brandi and I are doing a movie together, and I'm super excited about it. We should have more information for you in a few weeks."

Now tell me, Cassandra," said the MC, "you have conquered the big screen, the little screen, and the stage. What other surprises do you have in store for your fans?"

"Oh, I wouldn't dare answer that, darling. A lover must have some secrets, or what's the fun in being a lover? Now, tell me, Mr. Rollins, exactly how many rows are there on an ear of corn?"

This ambush question caught Lenora off guard. She grabbed the handrail to steady herself and tried to bark out an order but was too late. The MC had already begun answering. And he did it perfectly.

He said, "I'm afraid I'm not much of a farmhand, my love. Now, if you're looking for a man who knows how many diamonds are on a Rolex, then our future together looks very bright."

"Yes, I see," said Cassandra, with a smile. She then moved on down to the end of the red carpet to be escorted into the exhibit.

"That's a wrap, everyone," said Lenora. "You did a good job. Now go home and enjoy the rest of your weekend. Don't even bother shutting down. I'll take care of it for you."

Cass walked through the museum doorway and felt like she had walked right back into her mother's life. The exhibit displayed one of the sets from her mom's last movie. Cass had watched the movie a thousand times and had come to associate it with her mother's life in a thousand different ways. And now here it sat, in the real world, real enough to see and touch. The illusion had begun, and Cass wholeheartedly embraced it. She melted into her assigned seat—front row, center—and stared at the set.

The movie had been a breakout vehicle for her mom, a herald of better times to come. Against this backdrop of hope, Lenora's crime looked all the more terrible, but today Cass didn't care. She'd been transported back in time, and if the live portion of the exhibit had captured even a scintilla of the original magic, then Cass would soon be closer to her mom than she'd been since the day she had died.

Unlike the other exhibits Cass had seen, this one included traditional theater seating for about a hundred people. The setting for the scene depicted the dank and crowded storage basement under Zander McCreery's theater on Forty-Second Street in Manhattan. It looked like a storage area for a theater that over the years had collected more than its fair share of props, costumes, and set pieces. This included long bulging wardrobe racks and costumed mannequins stage left, hanging chandeliers and several rows of modular staircases stage right, and a jail cell at center stage.

The houselights dimmed. Cass's heart raced. And then she heard a voice that she loved. It belonged to her mother, as taken from the soundtrack of the movie. She played the role of Violet, and Cass listened as this part of the production played offstage.

Violet: *Here I am, Mr. McCreery. You called for me?*
McCreery: *Who are you again?*
Violet: *Violet Baker, fourth understudy for Hazel.*
McCreery: *Understudy! I don't need an understudy!*
Violet: *...and wardrobe assistant...*
McCreery: *That's what I need. Take these costumes down to the basement.*
Violet: *Yes, Mr. McCreery.*

The sound of a squeaky-wheeled costume rack echoed through the theater followed by the sound of a rattletrap elevator.

Violet then stepped onto the stage, and Cass's emotions galloped completely out of control. She tried to tell herself that she only saw a shadow...a mirage...but her mom looked so real, so alive. She wore a casual outfit consisting of a red-and-yellow-striped fitted midriff top, red high-waisted shorts, red-and-yellow ankle-strap wedges, and a blonde ponytail. It looked very 1950s and very sexy—as her mother had done so well at that time. Cass took a long, slow breath and tried to settle herself enough to enjoy her mom's performance.

A spotlight followed Violet as she pushed the costume rack over to the others at downstage left and mumbled dejectedly to herself. She said, "Understudy to Hazel-the-halfback. Might as well be understudy to a rock for all the good it will do me."

She suddenly grabbed a tattered straw hat from a nearby rack, put it on catawampus, and said, "Hi! My name's Hazel! I'm built like a tree stump and haven't missed a day of work since the hay cart ran me over!"

The audience laughed. Cass laughed through her tears.

Violet tossed away the hat and started transferring costumes from rack to rack. A particular gold-sequined evening gown caught her fancy. She held it up to admire and noticed a nearby mannequin dressed in a man's suit facing her direction. She showed him the dress and said, "What do you say, mister, can you see me in this? No? Well, that's just too bad because maybe I can see me in it." She quickly slipped on the gown over her clothes, pointed at the mannequin, and said, "And maybe I can see a whole lot more than this...if you care to know."

Cass joyously mouthed every word of dialogue. Now it came time for her mom to sing a song, a song that Cass knew very well because she and her mom had sung it a thousand times. Violet sang to the mannequin:

I see the top of the playbill, and maybe it's not so far

I see the lights on the marquee and the day you know you're a star
Camera flashes and cover stories and getting spotted on the street
Long lines and sold-out shows for a hundred dollars a seat
And Mister, if it's all the same
I can also see the day
When someone knows my name

Violet turned her attention back to the costume racks but soon heard a stirring. She looked up and saw that the mannequin had come to life. Violet became mesmerized. She slowly walked toward him. He sang:

Say there, pretty thing
Haven't I seen you somewhere before?
Onstage, on-screen
Or maybe you're just the checker at the grocery store

The man suddenly turned back into a mannequin. Violet looked disappointed. She gave him a knock on the shoulder, and he toppled over. She sang:

I can see fairy tales that never will be
Glass slippers and little red Martians
Pixie dust and wild hobgoblins
How come I can't see the fairy tale inside of me?

How come I can't see the fairy tale inside of me?

Violet spied another mannequin nearby. This one was dressed like a cop and had a hand out as if directing traffic. Violet faced him and sang:

I see a private dressing room, and my name is on the door
I see the hills of Hollywood and midnight flights from shore to shore
Hopeful actors and clever playwrights and money makers gather 'round
They wait in line behind the faithful autograph hound
And copper, if it's all the same
I can also see the day
When someone knows my name

This mannequin also came to life. Violet smiled. He sang:

Say there, pretty thing
You have a face that everyone knows
An actor, a singer
Or maybe you're just the waitress at Delmonico's

He turned back into a mannequin. Violet gave him a knock on the shoulder, and he toppled over. When she looked up, Violet saw another mannequin staring at her. Like the others, this one had come to life, but he didn't look as welcoming. He wore a top hat, tails, and penetrating black eyes. Black sideburns and a dark brow framed a stern countenance. Violet kept her distance and sang:

I can see fairy tales that never will be
Glass slippers and little red Martians
Pixie dust and wild hobgoblins
How come I can't see the fairy tale inside of me?
How come I can't see the fairy tale inside of me?

The dark-browed mannequin studied Violet for a second and then sang:

You say you can see
But you don't know what you are
A hopeless wannabe
Who's not even close to becoming a Broadway star

He held out his gloved hand. Violet hesitated, but only for a second. Then she walked up, put her hand into his, and they danced. They danced beautifully, perfectly, athletically—just as they had in the movie.

At that moment Cass wanted to jump out of her seat and rush the stage like an unhinged fan. She wanted to laugh hysterically and bounce in and out of their dance, tagging along step for step, up and down the staircases, over the fallen mannequins, in and out of the costume racks. She wanted to touch her mother, to smell her, to get scolded by her for such outrageous behavior. And at the end she wanted them all to fall into an exhausted heap and to laugh about how crazy it had been and about how they might just do it again the very next day.

Cass managed to stay in her seat, however, and the reward proved almost as satisfying as her fantasy. At the end of the dance, the dark man unfurled her mom and sent her pirouetting across the stage. She came to a dramatic stop. The music stopped. The two stared into each other's eyes for a second, and then the dark man sang:

Everyone has a dream
You need something more
Come back and see me when your dream is worth dying for
Come back and see me when your dream is worth killing for

"No! Please! Please don't go!" said Violet, as she rushed up to him. It was too late. The man had turned back into plastic. Violet knocked him on the shoulder, like the others, but he didn't fall. Instead, his gloved hand fell open and revealed a black business card. Violet took the card and read it. Then she sang:

I can see fairy tales that never will be
Glass slippers and little red Martians
Pixie dust and wild hobgoblins
Maybe I can see the fairy tale inside of me
Maybe I can see the fairy tale inside of me
Maybe I can see the fairy tale inside of me

Violet looked once more at the business card and then rushed offstage. The music swelled to a final crescendo, the stage went black, and the audience broke into enthusiastic applause. Cass choked back the tears and joined them. At that moment she loved Lenora's museum without reservation, like a child loves her mother.

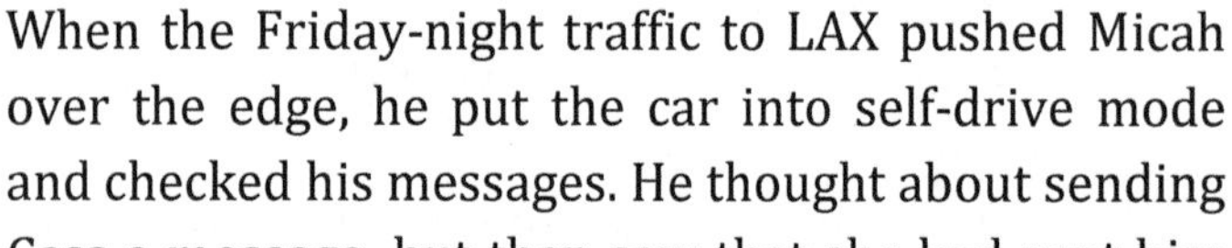

When the Friday-night traffic to LAX pushed Micah over the edge, he put the car into self-drive mode and checked his messages. He thought about sending Cass a message, but then saw that she had sent him one earlier that evening. She said, "Where are you?"

He texted back, "On my way to Florida. What do you think about getting together when I get back? P.S. You can't fool me. I know what you did. I went back and checked the film."

Then Micah thought about it. It kind of sounded like Cass had expected him to be somewhere. He scrolled up, through the various messages, to see if he had missed something, and found five recent messages that had been deleted. That didn't make any sense. First of all, he and Cass hadn't talked at all in the last week outside of work. Secondly, he hadn't deleted any messages.

Suddenly a very uneasy feeling washed over him, the kind of feeling that hit after he'd been ambushed by Lenora. He logged into the ranch's security system and checked the live feeds from the various cameras. Up at the museum he saw a parking lot full of cars, uniformed valets, and a red carpet leading up to the museum entrance. And he saw Cass's black BMW parked by the red carpet. He instantly understood what it meant: Lenora did have a scheme, and it included getting him out of town and getting Cass into the museum.

He quickly dialed Cass's number, but it went straight to a recording. He left an urgent, hysterical message. He also pounded out a quick text that said, *Don't go into museum. Leave. Leave now*! Then he jerked the car over to the emergency lane and stomped on the gas pedal.

Lenora, dressed in a glitter knit black evening gown, appeared from the wings down stage right. She welcomed the audience's reception with a modest smile and then stepped up to the microphone. She said, "Wendy Rainy's portrayal of Violet in *Zombies on Broadway* is a performance that should be remembered forever. And now it will be. We not only rescued it and restored it, but we have converted it back into the dynamic live performance that it was over sixty years ago. But the best part is that the world premiere of this reborn gem has been witnessed by Wendy Rainy's very own daughter, who, as you all know, is an accomplished actor in her own right. Please welcome our special guest, Cassandra Moreaux."

Cass rose from her seat, crossed over to the left, and stepped onto the stage. She and Lenora embraced. Lenora said, "Cassandra, what was it like to see this recreation of your mother's live performance?"

"Take a look at my mascara, and you'll have your answer," said Cass.

The audience laughed, but their timing felt out of sync, like someone had pushed a laugh-track button a half beat too late. Cass ignored it. She also ignored a quiet voice from somewhere in her soul that cautioned not to get carried away by emotion and to remember the pain that Lenora had caused as well as the punishment that she deserved. But the tribute to her mom felt too wonderful, and Cass didn't want to let it go. She wanted it to last forever and to be experienced by everyone. She said, "You have created a magical place, Lenora. And I hope I'm the first person to congratulate you and to say that you have my unwavering support and cooperation."

"Wouldn't it be great to see Cassandra perform with her mother?" said Lenora. The audience approved, and Lenora continued: "Well, I have a surprise for you. Visitors to this museum don't just watch. They participate. In a special performance created for this wonderful occasion, Cassandra and her mother will demonstrate this unique participation for you right now. Cassandra will be the guest who's been given this encoded card when she bought her ticket." Lenora held up one of the cards on a lanyard that Cass had seen before. Lenora then placed the lanyard around Cass's neck. She also offered to take Cass's handbag for safekeeping. Cass hesitated because it seemed strange. Then she handed it over anyway.

"With this special card, the guest is now welcomed into all the exhibits," said Lenora, "not just as an onlooker but also as a recognized member of the cast. Sit back and watch how fun and revolutionary this can be."

Lenora escorted Cass upstage to the jail cell. Cass didn't remember ever seeing a jail scene in any of her mother's movies. She stepped into the cell anyway, and lighting embedded into the floor started flashing. Lizard-green fluorescent words said, "You have talent! Step inside and show the world!" Cass stared at those words. The last time she had seen them, she got knocked flat by one of Lenora's android goons. The memory of that violent encounter rattled Cass's brain. It woke her up. It sounded the alarm. Something was not right. She turned to leave. Lenora slammed the cell door in her face.

Cass looked at Lenora, who stood just inches away on the other side of the bars. The showbiz smile had vanished, and her eyes had become two piercing lasers, focused and deadly.

Cass shook the door. It didn't budge. She said, "Unlock this door, Lenora. Right now."

Lenora said, "Greatness does not just rise up from the ashes. I can tell you that from personal experience. It is constructed over a lifetime, painfully, block by block, cut from sweat and blood. And, if necessary, from the dead bodies of your enemies."

Someone entered the stage. It was her mother, still dressed in the evening gown, but now she carried a black gun in her right hand. She stopped at center stage, just a few feet away, almost close enough to touch. She looked blankly at Cass. Cass looked at her.

"You will be performing with your mother, Cassandra," said Lenora. "It's a scene I wrote especially for you. It's called 'Mother Murders Daughter' and I hope you carry the memory of it all the way to hell."

Now Lenora's twisted fantasy became clear, and it did more than just frighten Cass. It repulsed her, made her want to look away from the android creation, away from the depravity. But like a disobedient dog pulling on a leash, her eyes continued to pull toward the image of her mother, and Cass didn't have the strength to resist. She looked. She looked at the face of an angel. She looked at the beautiful eyes of her one and only hero. But then she looked again at the gun, and the spell instantly shattered. In all her days, her mother had never come close to this kind of hatred. This imposter that now stood before Cass amounted to nothing but a sick killing machine, conceived and created by an evil mind.

Cass needed to think quickly. She said, "Lenora! Think about what you're doing! Think about what it will do to your museum! There are a hundred witnesses!"

"I'm not worried about them," said Lenora. "They have a really bad habit of dozing off at just the right time."

A barely audible hum echoed through the theater. It lasted a few seconds, and then the heads of everyone in the audience slumped forward. And Cass's heart slumped, too. She realized that the trap had been planned with meticulous Lenora Danmore precision.

"But then again," said Lenora, "they really do like a good murder. I think I'll let them stay up for this one."

The audience instantly awoke and clapped like someone had just guessed the right answer on a fun game show.

Cass fought back the panic that clawed at her heart and mind. She pleaded, "You don't have to do this, Lenora! You just heard me say that you have my complete support!"

"At a price I won't pay! This is not the Wendy Rainy Museum!" screamed Lenora, with wide eyes and a jabbing finger. "It is not a last gasp for mediocrity! It is the Lenora Danmore Museum, and my lifetime of discipline and dedication and excellence is the only reason it's even possible!"

Lenora had crossed over to psycho-land, and Cass didn't want to go there. She changed direction. "You won't get away with it, Lenora. I sent the file to my attorney. If anything happens to me, you will be exposed," she said.

Lenora took a deep, palsied breath and said, "I doubt it. Besides, I can deal with attorneys. They settle for money. Self-righteous daughters want blood. Goodbye, Cassandra. You have no one to blame but yourself." She stepped aside a few feet, looked at the android, and said, "You may begin, Wendy. Please take it from the top."

"Yes, Miss Danmore," said the android. Her face then instantly became animated. She raised the gun and pointed it at Cass. With a kindly smile, she said, "I'm so happy we get to share this moment together,

Cassandra. Is there anything you'd like to say before I kill you?"

Lenora leaned forward and whispered to Cass, "Your dialogue is projected onto the wall...in case you want to go out like a true professional."

Cass's eyes darted up to the wall. She had three lines before the end of the scene. She turned her attention to the android and the gun. Cass moved to one side of the cell and then to the other. The gun followed her every move.

"Say the line, Cassandra, and say it like you mean it, or the scene will end, and you will die right now," commanded Lenora.

Cass read the line, "Yes, Mother. I have a question. How did you get the part of Violet in *Zombies on Broadway*?"

Two lines to go. Cass clutched her arms to her body, as if in fear, and wrapped her fingers around the encoded card that hung from her neck.

"I took private acting lessons from the producer," said the android.

Cass read the next line: "You took many private lessons, all over town, but you never got top billing, did you, Mother?"

Lenora laughed.

Now only one line remained before the end. Cass gave a quick, short tug on the card. It popped free from the lanyard.

"Top billing doesn't belong to the weak, dear," said the android.

Cass read her last line, "Is that why you gave up and killed yourself?"

"No, dear, that's why I'm killing you," said the android. She then pulled back the hammer and aimed the gun at Cass's heart.

Cass tossed the card out of the cell. It hit Lenora's leg and landed on the floor by her feet.

The android swiveled and pointed the gun at Lenora. Lenora stared at her creation with wide, unbelieving eyes. The android fired two rapid shots. Lenora clutched her chest, stumbled for a step, and collapsed to the floor. Her arms and legs twitched for a few seconds and then stopped. The android stepped over to the lifeless body, bent over it, and said, "Good job, Cassandra. Keep up the good work. And do not forget to pick up a copy of our scene from the gift store. I think you will like it." Then her head slumped forward, and she powered down—as did the android audience.

Cass clutched the bars of the jail cell and slowly eased herself to the floor. She felt dizzy and lost. Her brain struggled to fathom how the unspeakable beauty she had witnessed just minutes earlier had instantly mutated into violence and death. Or maybe there had never been any beauty at all. Maybe her blind eye had foolishly believed what had never truly been seen. She tried to breathe, but her body refused to be governed. Confused, roiling emotions of the last forty-eight hours of her life, of hope, hatred, revenge, and forgiveness flooded her heart and soul. She lowered her head and cried.

After a few moments, Cass heard the sound of someone clapping, and then someone else, and someone else. She raised her head and, through the tears, saw the android audience on their feet applauding. Then, before Cass had time to understand what it meant, they fell in unison back into their seats and died to the world once again.

"You're a clever girl, Cassandra. It's too bad you didn't put it to good use. You could have been somebody," said a voice from across the theater.

Cass knew that voice. It had just been burned into her conscience and cued up for a lifetime of bad dreams. But it didn't make sense. She looked at the dead body on the floor—the dead body that was supposed to belong to Lenora. And then she saw it. There was no blood. There was no blood... Cass slowly turned toward the speaker, as if stealth caution might make the evil disappear. She saw Lenora walking down the center aisle between the seats. She wore a white lab coat and a face of stone. She climbed the steps to the stage, strode directly to the sleeping android, and pulled the gun from her fingers. Cass pulled herself to her feet.

Lenora stepped over to the cell door, pointed the gun at Cass's head, and said, "The year is 1951, and you have a choice between happiness and misery. What do you choose?"

Cass didn't say anything.

"There are no road signs. There is confusion and fear. What do you choose?" said Lenora.

"I choose not to stab my friend in the back," said Cass.

"Like you didn't stab Brandi Bonacore in the back?"

"I did that out of ignorance. You betrayed my mother to further your career. You had a choice."

"My name is Karolina Wojtkowiak! I am the immigrant daughter of a communist! I had no choice!" Lenora cocked the gun and continued: "When desperation wraps its fingers around your neck, everything changes. Look at you. An insignificant political storm rattled your cage, and look what you did. You call it ignorance. I call it a window to your soul, a dark and scary window, just like mine. The only difference is that I don't go halfway. I finish what I start."

Lenora steadied her aim. Cass huddled in the farthest corner of the cell, still just feet from the weapon. She closed her eyes. A loud pop echoed through the theater. Cass didn't feel any pain. She opened her eyes and saw Lenora looking up at the wall where the dialogue had been projected. She stared at a live video of herself and Cass and the gun. The popping had not been the sound of gunfire but the crackling sound of an audio-video system being turned on. Someone had turned on a camera.

Lenora turned and looked out over the audience. All the androids still had their heads down...except for one in the front row. He smiled and stared alertly. Lenora walked to the edge of the stage and shot him in the head. He slumped forward, and the video disappeared from the wall. Lenora returned to the cell. Without a word, she pulled back the hammer and thrust the gun through the bars. Once again a loud pop rang out, and once again Lenora's live image flashed onto the wall, just in time to catch an angry spasm course through her convulsed body, punctuated by a harrowing shriek of "I will not allow this!" A new android had raised his head.

Lenora stormed downstage, but this android sat several rows back and proved difficult to kill. She fired three times before the android slumped over and the video disappeared from the wall.

Just as Lenora turned and emerged from a cloud of gun smoke, Micah rushed from the wings. Cass let out a loud, uncontrolled gasp. Micah glued his eyes onto Lenora and slowly edged over to the cell, placing himself between Lenora and her victim.

Lenora walked toward Micah, gun at her side. She said, "Get out of here, Micah."

"Everything has been recorded, Lenora," said Micah, as he showed Lenora his phone. "All it takes is the push of a button and the world will see it."

God bless Micah and his nerdy phone, thought Cass.

Lenora moved in close enough to make an easy shot and slowly raised the gun.

"You know I will do it, Lenora," said Micah, with his finger on the button.

"And you know I will kill you," said Lenora.

"Yes, I do. But will you destroy your legacy? Will you destroy Lenora Danmore, the movie queen who is supposed to live forever?"

The outstretched gun shook in Lenora's hand. Her breathing sputtered. A tear rolled down her cheek, and she said, "She's already dead. All that's left now is revenge." She cocked the gun and aimed. "Goodbye, Micah. We never really bonded anyway. I think you might have a personality defect." Lenora pulled the trigger. And nothing happened except for a harmless click. She fired again with the same result, and then again.

Micah reached through the bars, pulled Cass close, and said, "Are you OK?"

"I'm OK," said Cass.

"This is not over!" bellowed Lenora. "You are nothing but a backlot Barbie! Do you hear me? I've taken down giants ten times bigger than you!" She reared back and hurled the gun at them. It clanked off an iron bar and dropped to the floor. "I will destroy you, Cassandra Moreaux, just like I destroyed you mother!" She charged the Wendy

Rainy look-alike, knocked it over, and stomped and kicked it.

Micah reached up to the top of the cell and flipped a lever. The cell door popped open. Cass looked at it and said, "Shit."

"It's a prop," said Micah. "Let's get out of here." He wrapped an arm around Cass and guided her to a backstage emergency exit.

The world looked completely different when Cass walked through that door. It looked fresh and new. A cool evening breeze gently swirled in the trees. The stars shimmered in the embrace of a velvety black sky. A long line of footpath lights laid down a ribbon of golden gauze, like a fairy-tale path for hobbits or leprechauns. Cass wondered at a world where beauty and danger marched in such close quarters. She had seen them that very night, death and life, patrolling the same side of the street, thinly separated by good and bad intentions. Truth might be just around the corner. Or it might be deceit. Or was it even possible to know the difference? Just now she had been rescued by a man who was supposed to have been her enemy. She turned a corner, saw his face, and enemy turned into friend as danger inexplicably turned into beauty.

Cass stopped in her tracks. She didn't have an answer for the kind of unmarked randomness that had just exploded in her face, but she had the next best thing. She needed to surround herself with as much goodness as possible. Everyone needed it because we might not be able to control what waits around the corner, but we sure as hell control who we're with when we get there. She turned to Micah and said, "Micah Bailey, I have something to tell you." Then she told him...with a kiss...about a thousand words' worth.

"I like the way you talk," said Micah.

"You should see me when I get really chatty."

"I'd like that."

"But I think we'll start with the small talk...which reminds me, you're supposed to be in Florida. How did you know?"

"It's what I do," said Micah. "I get paid to stay one step ahead."

"Well, Micah Bailey, you're good at what you do. But to tell the truth, your job sucks."

CHAPTER SEVENTEEN

Early the next morning Micah clutched the doorknob on the back entrance to one of the exhibits. He'd decided that leaving without a word didn't feel right. But now he had second thoughts. He wondered why he didn't turn around and make a clean exit. What flaw drove him forward, like a car that keeps driving on a flat tire? Then he heard the familiar, angry voice, and he pushed through the doorway and walked toward it, just as he had every day for the last twenty-five years. He found a seat in the shadows and watched.

Lenora stood in the middle of the set next to a dusty covered wagon that had a broken wheel and torn canopy. Big boulders that looked like they hadn't been touched by a drop of rain in ten years littered the landscape. The sun-bleached skeletal remains of a dead animal splayed out in the dirt off to the side. Lenora wore a blue prairie dress, a bonnet, and lace-up boots—an identical costume to the one she'd worn sixty years earlier while in her twenties. It hurt to even look at her now.

Micah knew the movie well. The first time, as a ten-year-old, he'd stumbled upon it while flipping TV channels. He then had closed the door and turned down the volume. He didn't want his dad to know that he cared. Back then, on that afternoon rerun, he had seen beauty and strength. His yearning imagination added compassion and tenderness and other motherly standbys. Now every bit of it, real and imagined, had vanished, and only rancid ambition and the feebleness of old age remained.

Lenora had a lanyard around her neck and had been yelling at the android director, who stood next to her. She continued, "Listen to me! Listen to what I am saying! He cannot pause on that line because it kills my motivation for the entire scene! Do you understand what I am saying?"

The kindly director smiled and said, "Good job, Miss Danmore. Keep up the good work. And do not forget to pick up a copy of your scene from the gift store. I think you will like it."

Lenora slapped him across the face and screamed, "You will not use that cut!"

The android tried to sputter out a few words but then gave up and powered down. His head slumped forward.

"You stupid, stupid man!" shrieked Lenora.

Micah closed his eyes, not just because he found it difficult to look at but also because he found it difficult to look at himself. It had finally ended. Cass had crushed Lenora. And yet here he sat the next morning, hovering in the darkness, hoping for a goodbye. He'd never gotten a hello, but maybe if he behaved like a good boy, he'd get a goodbye. He had become a forty-three-year-old urchin begging for crumbs.

He pulled the big ring of ranch keys from his pocket and set them on the bench. But when he stood up, something disturbed the keys, and they fell loudly to the floor. Lenora's head shot up, and her eyes met Micah's. She stared at him, and he stared at her. And then she turned her back.

She didn't say a single word, and that tiny fact spoke volumes—even if they had never had anything else, they had always had words. They had a towering mountain of them. But truthfully, all those words over all those years had never rightfully belonged to either one of them. They had never been about them or for them or against them. The words had always been about the glorious project. Those words had built an empire of projects and nothing else. But now the last project had ended, and all the words had run out. Lenora didn't even have enough to fire him one last time, and Micah didn't have enough to fashion one last barb.

He left the exhibit, made the short walk to the workshop, and opened the doors one last time. As he passed by his desk, the picture of his ex-wife stared up at him. He picked it up, looked at it for a few seconds, and then put it back on the desk, facedown. He had failed her, and some failures can never be undone. He could only do his best to make sure it never happened again.

He looked around the workshop at his life's accumulation and didn't have the least inclination to scoop things up and carry them away. This life had been a slow-dripping poison, and he was done with it. He had the suitcase he'd packed the previous day for Florida, and that's all he needed...except...for a certain car. It happened to be an unusual babe magnet for an unusual babe.

He opened the doors to the car museum, flipped on the lights, and smiled at the sorry-looking, roofless, burned-out wreck from *Planes, Trains & Automobiles.* Any woman who could love this car had to be something very special. He threw his suitcase into the backseat, fired it up, and drove out the museum's giant roll-up door and down the hill to Cass's trailer. He pushed on the horn. It didn't work, so he whistled. Cass emerged with a suitcase in each hand. She approached with a sly smirk and, in a deep voice, said, "Excuse me, mister. Do you really believe that this vehicle is safe to drive?"

"Yes, ma'am, I do. I really do," said Micah.

"Well, that's good enough for me. Let's go!" She put her suitcases next to Micah's and hopped into the car. After a few seconds, she said, "Where are we going?"

"I don't know," said Micah. "I thought maybe I'd give Hollywood a try. Do you think they have room for a smart-ass game-show host?"

"You know, I heard there's a shortage of those right now. You might just be in luck."

Micah welcomed his passenger with a long kiss. He then shoved down on the gear shifter. The gears grinded out a loud protest, and the unsightly hulk wobbled down the driveway, off the ranch, and into the golden California sunshine.

The End

ACKNOWLEDGEMENTS

This endeavor would not have been possible without the faithful support of my wife, Martina. I'm proud and thankful to be her partner.

THE AUTHOR

Tim Patrick is a graduate of UCLA. He and his wife live in Southern California and are the parents of two grown children. In his spare time, he enjoys aviation, mountain biking, and experimenting in the kitchen, where he is an undisputed connoisseur of the tater tot.

CPSIA information can be obtained
at www.ICGtesting.com
Printed in the USA
LVHW05s1958210618
581512LV00013B/520/P